WANTON HEAT

Nicola Marsh

Zoe Keaton's bad-girl reputation is renowned for landing her in trouble. So when her job is on the line and she travels to Italy to land a vital business deal, she has to rein in every natural instinct to flirt with royalty.

Enigmatic Prince Dominic Ricci has no intention of listening to her pitch, but Zoe never gives up. With the queen's help she does whatever it takes to get the job done. Including kidnapping the prince!

However, she doesn't count on the matchmaking queen's interference stranding Zoe and Dominic on the royal family's secluded island.

Zoe can't afford to mix business with pleasure. She must prove she's more than an entitled rich girl who bought her way to success. But who can resist a sexy prince and when Dominic turns on the charm the latent chemistry between them ignites.

Zoe knows it's just a sizzling fling...or can a gorgeous Italian prince hiding a tragic past fall for a girl like her?

Copyright © Nicola Marsh 2014
Published by Nicola Marsh 2017

All the characters, names, places and incidents in this book have no existence outside the imagination of the author and have no relation whatsoever to anyone bearing the same name or names and are used fictitiously. They're not distantly inspired by any individual known or unknown to the author and all the incidents in the book are pure invention. Any resemblance to actual events, locales, or persons, living or dead, is coincidental.

All rights reserved including the right of reproduction in any form. The text or any part of the publication may not be reproduced or transmitted in any form without the written permission of the publisher.

The author acknowledges the copyrighted or trademarked status and trademark owners of the word marks mentioned in this work of fiction.

(Originally published under the same title by Entangled Publishing in February 2014.)

Chapter One

Zoe Keaton had never conformed a day in her life.

At nine months, she'd defied the coddling of her parents and walked.

At three, she'd ridden her tricycle straight through a stained-glass window in their Texan mansion, because they'd told her not to go too fast.

At ten, she'd run away twice, because they wouldn't allow her to get a Mohawk and a nose ring, in that order.

By the time she'd hit puberty, her mom had given up on her, her dad indulged his "wild child," and she'd been the coolest kid in school.

Zoe liked being a rebel. It suited her. Which made having to schmooze some uptight, surly, silver-spoon up-his-ass Italian prince for business all the harder.

Zoe wasn't a monarchist. She was an anarchist.

And the only prince she had any respect for was the Artist Formerly Known As, one of her dad's vintage faves. Though Prince William was kinda cute. She really liked the way those tight white polo britches highlighted a guy's assets.

That's about the only thing Prince Dominic Ricci of Osturo—a tiny Italian island off the coast of Naples—had going for him. His assets. And she wasn't talking about the modern sandstone castle she could see at the end of a long stone-flagged driveway.

She'd researched the prince online. Several times. Just to make sure she was fully equipped to convince Prince Pompous-Pants that the ad campaign she'd devised for the resort on one of his other islands, Ancora, was just what his kingdom needed. She'd busted her ass working on a contemporary campaign for the outdated resort, which was owned by her company's new lucrative client Kai Kaluna. Though she could've achieved her research objective with one session. Instead, she'd taken one look at the prince and bookmarked him.

His Lordship was hot. Seriously hot. The type of hot that made a girl want to find a dark-haired, blue-eyed look-alike and ride him until dawn.

It was a shame she'd sworn off flings for a while. She could've had fun flirting with a prince. What was the point of spending a week in a castle on a gorgeous Italian island in the Mediterranean if she couldn't indulge in some hot island nights?

But having a fling with the guy she had to do business with was a disaster waiting to happen. She'd already messed up enough recently. Hell, she'd almost made AW Advertising, the company she co-owned, go under because of her gung-ho approach with their oldest clients. The company's most valuable clients had walked, thanks to her. And what had she done? Rather than telling her BFF and co-owner Allegra Wilks the truth, she'd accepted a partnership as a step toward making amends.

Zoe saw it as her penance. With the constant doubts plaguing her after that spectacular failure, she needed to land this ad campaign for Kai Kaluna to prove she was more than a trumped-up Texan-turned-Californian who couldn't achieve anything without the safety net of Daddy's new money behind her.

As for failing again and potentially pissing off Kaluna... if he walked and took his business with him, AW Advertising would be finished. They'd be screwed, and she'd be the one personally responsible.

No way would she let that happen. And that meant schmoozing a prince with bedroom eyes and a sardonically sexy smile.

Fan-fricking-tastic. The last thing she needed to be reminded of before her all-important first meeting with the prince was how hot the guy was. Bad enough she had to curb another impulse to check out that bookmarked Google page on him again before seeing him in the flesh.

Flesh...hard, bronzed, and ripped, from those pics she'd seen online...

Don't go there, dumbass.

She shook her head, clasped her handbag tighter, hoisted her overnight bag higher on her shoulder, and followed the cobblestoned path toward the castle entrance. Like her mistaken assumption of the prince, whom she'd envisaged as being middle-aged, grim, and flabby, she'd imagined the castle to be a crumbly pile of old rocks.

Both her preconceptions had been blown sky-high. The L-shaped, three-story sandstone building perched on a cliff top overlooking incredible expanses of indigo Tyrrhenian Sea appeared as modern as its owner. Beautiful arched windows, immaculate manicured lawns, and an ash wood front door that would be monstrous up close.

Okay, so the fact that she had to stay here for seven days wasn't all bad. If she could get the prince on board and her work done, maybe she could play princess in her downtime.

The thought of her lounging around a castle made her stumble, and she dropped her overnight bag. She bent to retrieve it, and when she straightened, the thing slipped out of her hand again.

Fricking hell.

Less than four feet away, dripping water onto the flagstones, stood the most gorgeous male specimen she'd ever seen.

Bare, bronzed chest glistening in the sun. Rivulets of water trickling toward a loosely knotted towel slung low on his hips. Long, lean legs. Muscled.

She dragged her gaze upward to the sizable bulge beneath the towel...

"Fuck." The expletive slipped out before she could stop it.

Not exactly how she'd imagined her first word to Prince Dominic Ricci.

He quirked an eyebrow. "Something the matter?"

Zoe had one second to redeem herself. She could flounder and apologize and grovel. But she'd end up looking more like a fool. So she did what she did best. Revert to type. "Nothing's wrong." She deliberately looked him up and down, trying her best not to linger on that towel. "In fact, all seems right with the world from where I'm standing."

His other imperious eyebrow joined the first. "Do I know you?"

"Would you like to?"

Crap, she was flirting with royalty. Could they behead her for doing this?

To her relief, the corners of his lips curved upward. "You're American."

"Don't hold that against me." She resisted the urge to shuffle her feet under the intensity of his stare. "Born and bred Texan, but an LA girl at heart."

He wrinkled his nose as if she'd presented him with a pile of doggy doo. "Flashy and fake."

She puffed up in indignation. "Now hang on a minute—"

"The city, not you."

This time it was his turn to do the surveying, and he started at her coral-painted toes and inched upward, his stare lingering on her calves, her knees, her hips. She'd opted for a sedate black-and-white fitted maxi-dress to meet the prince, but by the way her skin tingled? There was nothing sedate about his perusal.

She dragged in a breath, which drew his attention to her breasts. By the time he locked gazes with her, she could've sworn her heart had stopped. She'd had her fair share of sex, had flirted and seduced, but no guy had ever made her feel so...*wanton* with just a look.

"You're beautiful," he said, closing the small distance between them. "But I think you already know that?"

Zoe would have usually thrust out her boobs and responded with an "abso-fricking-lutely." But there was something about this guy that made her strangely tongue-tied.

She shrugged, as if his compliment meant little. "I've had my fair share of flattery from guys willing to do anything to get what they want."

"And what do you think I want, *cara*?"

Oh, boy. Courtesy of her crash course in Italian—the native language of Osturo—via her electronic tablet on the plane, he'd called her "darling."

In response to his semi-naked state, proximity, and polished Oxford accent with an underlying hint of his Italian background, she clenched her thighs together to prevent herself from collapsing at his feet and yelling, "Take me now."

Squaring her shoulders, she flashed him her most dazzling smile. "Why don't you tell me what you want?"

"Defiance in one so beautiful." He touched her cheek with a fingertip. "Enchanting."

As he trailed his fingertip toward her mouth, that simple touch short-circuited Zoe's common sense. She had no idea if it was the surrealism of the situation, the scent of lemon blossoms in the air, the heat of his touch, or the yearning in his eyes, but she found herself taking a step forward so their bodies were an inch apart.

She could feel the heat radiating off him, could smell an intoxicating blend of sea and sun and sexy male. And she couldn't resist...

She touched him.

Her palm splayed against his chest, her hand small and insignificant against that bronze expanse. He didn't move, but his fingertip continued its leisurely exploration of her face. So she explored, too. Her palm slid lower, gliding across his wet skin, tracing every tempting contour. She heard his harsh intake of breath as her fingers skated close to the knot of the towel.

And that's when she felt it. His hard-on nudging her hip. Zoe bit back a moan and dragged her gaze away from his chest. She couldn't do this. Not when so much rested on this deal going through.

"*Cara?*" His fingertip finally reached her bottom lip, where it lingered.

She would give anything to suck it into her mouth, to show him exactly what she wanted to do to him elsewhere.

Instead, she reluctantly stepped away.

The intimate spell enveloping them shattered when she glanced up and met his cold, steely glare.

"I was wondering how far you would go for your business proposition." He spat the last two words, making it sound like she wanted to assassinate him.

Realization washed over her, with a healthy dose of humiliation thrown in for good measure.

He'd been baiting her? What a prick.

"Not as far as you'd like, obviously." She pointedly stared at the front of his tented towel. "Or does that work on command like the rest of your serfs around here?"

The second the fiery comeback spilled from her lips, Zoe wished she could take it back. She shouldn't taunt him, not when she needed him so badly. Needed his business, that is. Whatever.

Amusement flickered in those unfairly piercing blue eyes. "I test everyone who sets foot in my domain. Don't take it personally."

His domain? Oh, yeah, the next seven days would be peachy good fun. She could see it now: him snapping his fingers, expecting her to jump to his tune. As if.

"Zoe Keaton." She stuck her hand out, the sensible greeting she should've delivered moments ago.

"From AW Advertising." He made it sound as if she planned on opening a full-service brothel in the castle foreground as he shook her hand so quickly, she could've imagined it. "We've been expecting you."

Was he using the royal pronoun or referring to a welcoming party that hadn't shown up yet?

Hating how off-kilter he made her feel, she gestured at his torso. "In that case, you're a tad underdressed."

"Didn't seem to bother you before," he murmured, a flare of heat sparking the indigo of his eyes before he cleared his throat. "I expected you to be waiting inside the castle, not strolling the grounds hoping to accost me."

"You wish," she muttered, biting back a grin as a frown creased his brow. "My ferry docked early, so I apologize. If I'd been on time, you would've had plenty of opportunity to cover up all of that."

She only just managed to avert her greedy gaze from the towel and *all of that*.

"Shall we?" He gestured for her to walk in front of him. "My grandmother will be waiting."

"Lead the way," Zoe said, eager to meet Queen Catarina Ricci, the figurehead matriarch who deferred everyday decisions to her grandson.

From Zoe's research, she'd learned that the queen had been a rebel in her day, traipsing through Europe, partying from one end to the other. She'd married for love, had bucked tradition by raising equally free-spirited children, and continued to host lavish parties that drew A-listers from around the world. And despite losing her three sons, including Dominic's dad, Franco, who'd died in a freak avalanche, she was renowned for her hospitality.

Too bad Catarina's grandson hadn't inherited some of his gran's social graces.

"You're wasting your time, you know." He held out his hand for her overnight bag. "Nothing you say will convince me to allow Kaluna to make Ancora a focal point for thousands to desecrate."

"I've got a week to change your mind." She gripped her bag tighter, despite her shoulder aching from the load. "Your grandmother obviously sees the potential of positive PR for this region, and she insisted I stay seven days to explore all the possibilities an ad campaign for a rejuvenated resort could provide."

He said something like "crazy Nonna" under his breath. "My grandmother is progressive for her age, but in the matter of promoting this region? We greatly differ."

"I like your grandmother already," Zoe said, glad to have at least one ally in her quest.

"And she's going to love you," he muttered, before rushing on. "Give me the bag."

His command rankled. "Why? So you can snap your fingers and have some poor servant pop out from behind a tree to do your bidding?"

To her surprise, he laughed, a genuinely happy sound that did something strange to her chest. "You're very outspoken."

"It's how I've always been." She squared her shoulders, as if daring him to disagree. "I'm blunt and persistent and outrageous, but I get the job done." She jabbed a finger in his direction. "Something you'll see very soon."

He muttered something in Italian that sounded distinctly derogatory. "The faster you hand over that bag, the faster you can start *convincing* me to ruin these islands all in the name of progress."

"And the faster you realize your islands are financially imploding along with the rest of the Italian economy, the faster you'll use your business brain to see that what I'm proposing can only benefit everyone." She hoisted the bag higher and tried not to wince as her shoulder pinched.

"You're right, you are blunt and persistent." He scowled. "But you forgot to add 'pain in the ass' to the list of your dubious attributes."

"You didn't seem to find my *attributes* so repugnant five minutes ago." She thrust out her chest for good measure in a purely childish "so there." The part where her nipples hardened beneath his potent stare kinda undermined the point she'd been trying to make.

WANTON HEAT

"Bag. Please?" He softened his command this time, and she didn't know what was worse. The way she couldn't stop staring at his bare chest, or the way his cajoling manner made her feel a little gooey inside.

"Fine." She handed the bag over, silently cheering at not having to lug the thing around any more. "While we're listing attributes, why don't we come up with a few for you?" She snapped her fingers. "Let's start with domineering and demanding."

He shrugged. "Valuable in my line of work."

"What work's that? Ordering subordinates to do your bidding or polishing the crown jewels?"

The second the retort popped out, Zoe wished she could take it back. She hadn't meant it the way it sounded, because when guys "polished" their "crown jewels"...ah, hell. She may as well re-board the ferry and head back to Naples now.

She heard a stifled snort, and when she shot him a quick sideways glance, he wore the smug grin of a guy who wasn't going to let her get away with that one.

"Polishing the crown jewels can be a lot of fun," he said, his grin widening as she picked up the pace a little. Maybe if she broke into a run, she could ditch him completely.

"I'll take your word for it." She tilted her nose higher, knowing it was way too late for aloofness now.

"Maybe you'd like to help—"

"Stop right there." She came to an abrupt halt and held up her hand. "We need to clear the air."

She jerked a thumb over her shoulder. "What happened back there when we first met? A mistake."

She waved her hand between them. "You and me? We're both strong personalities used to getting our own way. So stands to reason we're going to butt heads and verbally spar for the next week."

Intrigue darkened his eyes to midnight. "Go on."

"I'm a natural flirt. It's my thing. But you..." She shook her head. "You're the prince of Osturo, and as long as you don't agree to my business proposal, you're also the enemy. So quit trying to unnerve me with your hot and cold act, and your lame-ass innuendoes, got it?"

Before he could respond, she pointed to his chest. "And for fuck's sake, put some clothes on."

She expected him to bristle or glower or order her the hell off his property. Instead, he tilted his head, as if studying her, before giving her a brisk nod.

"If your presentation is as interesting as you, guess it wouldn't hurt to hear you out."

With another deliberately insolent stare that swept her from head to foot, he strode away, leaving her with a tantalizing view of a firm ass she yearned to kick. Hard.

Chapter Two

While their houseguest freshened up, Dominic paced the rooftop conservatory.

When he'd been a child needing to escape the adult cheek-pinchers at the many lavish parties his parents hosted, he'd head for this room. Perched on the third floor at the farthest corner of the west wing, it had the best views of the island and surrounding ocean. And on a clear day, if he squinted really hard, he swore he could see his favorite place on the planet.

Ancora.

He'd traveled the world many times, had spent several years studying economics at Oxford and later living in London, but no place was home like Ancora.

As a young boy, the weekends his parents would whisk him away there were the happiest of his life, and later, in his teens, he'd make time to chill there whenever he needed R&R. He'd spent a week there after his parents' death, and a month after Lilia's. Grieving. Remembering. Forgiving.

It was his sanctuary.

And if Zoe Keaton had her way, it would be swarming with tourists.

Merda.

He continued pacing, oblivious to the polished marble-tiled floor and massive arched windows that let in the light from dawn to dusk, only pausing to stab at a button to open the retractable roof that brought the outdoors in. He liked that, the feeling of not being boxed in and confined. Freedom.

He yearned for it. A life without the heritage of hundreds of years dogging his every decision. But if the tragedy of the last five years had taught him anything, it was no use wishing for life to be different. He had to cope with the hand he'd been dealt and get on with the job. The job of ensuring that Osturo, his birthplace, and the adjoining island that his family owned, Ancora, prospered.

He'd been doing a shitty job of it so far, but that was all about to change according to that brazen American woman who'd strutted onto the castle grounds as if she were the queen instead of Catarina.

He should've known she was trouble the moment he caught sight of her blatantly ogling him. He should've given her marching orders. She was just like everyone else who entered his sphere: she wanted something.

In her case, she planned to bring tourists to Ancora. Yeah, like he'd allow that to happen. Destroying such a beautiful part of the world was sacrilege, even if he hadn't made a promise to himself to maintain it as is. His father's plans for the islands had been simple: preserve their pristine beauty, especially that of wild Ancora. And in honor of his dad's memory, Dominic hadn't touched a thing. He owed his father that much. So Kaluna's proposed expansion and worldwide ad campaign? Not going to happen.

But because of the way she'd sparked his sexual interest, for an insane moment he'd wished she were different, that she didn't want something from him. He'd endured schemers his entire life and had learned over the years that people would go to any lengths to get what they wanted.

Oxford students who'd sucked up to him for entry into his world. London businessman who'd done the same. Women at parties who deliberately targeted him in the hope of gaining more than a bed partner for the night.

He'd learned to protect himself well, discounting his disastrous engagement to Lilia.

Now, a bold, attractive woman had stormed his castle, wanting something he wasn't prepared to give. He should've definitely thrown her out. Instead, he'd flirted with her, and his cock had joined the party.

He'd deliberately gone for an ocean swim half an hour before her scheduled arrival, wanting to keep her waiting. He liked his adversaries off guard. But his plan had gone awry when she'd been early, and he'd been caught with his pants down. Literally.

He hadn't expected her to be so...so...bold. The way she'd looked at him, the way she'd touched him...damn, he was hard just thinking about it.

The sooner he heard what she had to say and he sent her on her way, the better. He had no intention of letting her stay a week, despite what his meddling Nonna wanted. Zoe could check out Kaluna's resort on Ancora, then take the ferry straight back to Naples.

And in the meantime, he'd get a PI he often used in business dealings to investigate Kaluna's plans for Ancora. Better to be prepared than blindsided. After Lilia's treachery? He'd never make that mistake again.

He slid his smartphone out of his suit jacket pocket, found the PI's details, and fired off an e-mail.

No way would anyone take him for a fool again.

"I saw you chatting to our guest earlier." His grandmother strode into the room, a nimble seventy-five and as mentally sharp as anyone half her age. "What's she like?"

He gritted his teeth against the urge to blurt exactly what he thought of Zoe Keaton. "She's pushy and obnoxious."

"She's also beautiful." Catarina took a seat at a wrought iron table, poured herself a glass of water, and added a slice of lemon. "Smart too, if she has you this wound up."

He accepted the glass of water she poured for him and sat opposite. "We need to be on good terms with the Kaluna Resort, and that's the only reason I'll meet her."

"Yet you're agreeing to let her stay a week?" Catarina tapped her bottom lip, pretending to ponder, while Dominic ignored that telltale matchmaking gleam in her eyes. "Interesting."

"I only allowed that because you blackmailed me into it." He shook his head. "If you don't let your cardiologist check you over more regularly, I'll kill you myself."

Catarina tsk-tsked. "Don't waste your Italian theatrics on me." She grinned. "Save your zeal for someone who deserves it, someone like our pretty visitor—"

"Nonna..." His warning fell on deaf ears as she reached over and patted his hand.

"Darling boy, I haven't seen you look so...riled in a long time." She squeezed his hand and released it. "It means this woman has sparked something inside you. A passion that has been lacking for too long—"

"It's business, Nonna, nothing more." He had to interrupt, before she ventured into territory he'd rather avoid.

He knew she meant well, but on the rare occasion Catarina brought up the subject of his dead fiancée and how he'd lost the love of his life, it took all his willpower not to blurt the sorry truth. His grandmother had been through enough pain in losing her sole surviving son a few years ago—no point adding to it. Besides, speaking ill of the dead would gain nothing. Best to leave the past in the past and hope to God he never made the same mistakes again.

"You spend too much time focusing on business." She tut-tutted. "These islands don't have to be your responsibility. Allowing Kaluna to increase tourism will allow you the freedom to explore your other ventures overseas and—"

"I'm not going anywhere, so stop trying to get rid of me."

Dominic knew the archaic royalty system that once dominated these islands was obsolete. The Italian government had more influence than he ever would. But the Ricci family owned land on Osturo and Ancora—a lot of it—and no matter how outdated the royals were here, his father had wanted to maintain the tradition of doing what was best for the people of the islands. So that's what he would do, too.

But he didn't want to argue with Catarina, either. His grandmother had doted on Franco, her eldest son, and Dominic wanted to make her proud of him, too. She deserved that much for the hardships she'd faced.

It had been bad enough she'd suffered two heart attacks following his father's death. He didn't want her having a third one that could prove fatal. He'd seen a few worrying signs lately: her occasional pallor and an increasing frequency of angina that she tried valiantly to hide. And despite her reassurances, he wanted her to have more regular checkups.

"Well, if you're not leaving the island to go in search of a little fun, maybe the fun can come to you." She raised her glass in a silent cheer as he struggled not to think about how much fun Zoe Keaton might be.

The woman was a menace, but he had to admit, she was an exceptionally sexy menace. The type of woman to make a man forget his past. A woman who could make a man forget his own damn name.

She was not his type. But for several long minutes in the gardens earlier, he'd almost wished she could be.

"Nonna, how many poor saps have you tried to pair up on this island over the years?"

Catarina screwed up her brow, pretending to think. "Hmm...let me see. Six marriages. Four engagements. And several very happy tourist hookups—"

"You need to stop trying to fix me up." He bit back a grin at her wounded expression. Truth was, his nonna was more famous for her role as matchmaker on Osturo than she was as a figurehead queen. "It never ends well."

Catarina pouted. "Maybe because you're so closed off you won't let any woman close. Maybe those cool blondes you prefer, the ones I've tried to set you up with, aren't right for you. Maybe I should find a different type of woman for you. Someone to challenge you. Someone like Z—"

"You should stop meddling in my personal life and concentrate on more important things, like your health."

He pointed at her heart. "You're seeing that cardiologist in Naples next month if I have to kidnap you to do it."

Catarina huffed and crossed her arms. "I said I would, if you let Zoe see Ancora so she can refine her campaign over the next week, listen to what she has to say, and keep an open mind."

He nodded. "I'll listen to her business proposal, organize a tour of Ancora with one of the guides, then send her back to the mainland." He thumped the table for emphasis. "That's it."

"Sounds like you have it all planned out." Catarina finished her drink, set her glass on the table, and stood. "I'll let you have your meeting in peace."

She paused at the doorway and glanced over her shoulder. "But don't forget what I said." She turned away, but not before Dominic heard her murmur, "You need to start living again."

Dominic had a life. Not the one he'd envisioned, but a life nonetheless.

A life under serious threat of being disrupted by a beautiful, tousle-haired blonde with a lush mouth and sinful eyes.

Dio mio.

The sooner he kicked her cute ass off his island, the better.

Chapter Three

Zoe could get used to this.

She padded into the bedroom, her bare feet leaving water smears. If the rain shower in the lavish, pale-gold marble bathroom had been impressive, it had nothing on the guest room she'd been assigned for the next week.

It was divine. From the ice-blue walls to the cool ivory marble-tiled floor, from the mini-chandelier to the cherub-embossed cornices, every item in the room had exquisite attention to detail. Classy without being overbearing. She'd bet Catarina was behind the decor. As for the king-size bed covered in opulent cream sheets offset by plump turquoise cushions, she could spend her entire time in here alone.

She'd been so wrong about this place, it wasn't funny. Her research suggested Osturo wasn't in major financial strife like the rest of Italy but the monarchs were figureheads not moving with the times. Thank goodness they'd modernized the castle. Light flooded the palace from the many floor-to-ceiling arched windows along the corridors leading to the guest wing, and her quarters were the epitome of style and elegance, not dreary and old-fashioned like she'd expected. What else had she been wrong about?

Not the surly prince, that's for sure. She may have seen glimpses of a guy willing to have a little fun if the mood struck, but when he'd accused her of using her sexuality to get ahead, his coldness and instant withdrawal had confirmed what she'd expected: he was a somber recluse too stuck in the past to move his country into the future.

She planned on changing all that.

Her cell buzzed in her bag, and she dug it out, her quick glance at the screen an instant reminder of exactly why she was on this island.

Work.

Zoe swiped the answer button with her thumb and held the cell to her ear. "Hey, babe. How's life on the Whitsunday Islands?"

"Just perfect." Allegra Wilks, her BFF and partner at AW Advertising, sighed. "Was a brilliant idea, taking two weeks off after the launch of Kaluna's new resort here. Jett and I...well, we're..."

"Having sex on the beach? Doing the horizontal kangaroo hop?"

Allegra didn't laugh as Zoe expected. Instead, she cleared her throat. "What I was trying to say is, Jett and I are engaged."

Zoe squealed and hoped she wouldn't get arrested for disturbing the peace by some security guard strolling the castle corridors. "Oh my God, that's freaking brilliant. Congrats, hon, I'm thrilled for you."

And she was, so where was the sliver of sadness coming from? Zoe liked being single. She'd made it into an art form. "Treat 'em mean; keep 'em keen" had been her motto forever. She didn't do relationships or emotional entanglements or any of that sappy shit. She'd seen firsthand with her parents what that could do to a woman, and no way would she be any guy's doormat. So why the fleeting yearning for there to be more to life than dating, parties, and transient sex?

"I know it's crazy, because we've only known each other a few months, but I love him so much, Zo-Zo," Allegra said, her joy audible. "Go on, tell me I'm nuts."

Usually, Zoe would. She'd tease her reserved friend unmercifully. She'd done it all through college, when geeky Allegra would rather hide away in their dorm and study than attend frat parties. She'd done it when Allegra had first launched AW Advertising in LA, and Zoe had insisted on a role as her personal assistant rather than a partner despite an equal monetary start-up investment. And she'd done it all through Allegra's engagement to that wiener Flint, her Hollywood producer ex.

But Allegra was finally happy. Zoe had never seen two people more in love, and she didn't have it in her to rib her BFF over this. Besides, she had to wrap up this call so she could go meet the prince and coerce him into entering a mutually beneficial financial arrangement for them all. And ensure that she proved she could handle the responsibility of co-running a company to make up for the complete screw-up she'd made of it in LA.

Making this deal happen was imperative.

She may have left her home in Texas a long time ago, but she'd never forgotten the condescending stares, the deliberate taunts, because she came from "new" money. Her dad had flaunted his oil-subsidized wealth while she'd shunned it.

It was the sole reason she'd wanted to be a PA when Allegra first started up AW Advertising. She hadn't wanted to buy her way into the company just because of the money. She'd wanted to prove herself, to work her way to the top.

And look how that had turned out.

No way would she botch this deal. Kaluna Resorts had chosen AW to deliver on a promise, and that's what Zoe intended to do.

Failure wasn't an option.

"Oh my God, you're too quiet, which is so not you," Allegra said. "So you must definitely think I'm nuts. Shit."

"You're not nuts, babe," Zoe said, unable to resist her impish side for long. "You're just sexed up, and it's turned you into a romantic schmuck."

Allegra laughed. "Hey, you've been getting it on a lot longer than me over the years. I'm just making up for lost time."

"Getting it on?" Zoe snorted. "What are you, fifty?"

"Fifty times this week and counting." Allegra snickered. "Jealous?"

"Make it a hundred, and you'll come close to one of my quiet weeks," Zoe said, enjoying how much her friend had loosened up since she'd met Jett. Hooking up with the laid-back Aussie had been the best thing to happen to Allegra in a long time.

"I'm not sure whether to scold you for bragging or hang up now, so I can go haul Jett off the reef, rip off his snorkeling gear, and try to beat your record."

"You know I'm full of crap," Zoe said, waving to a security guard strolling the outer perimeter of the garden. He glowered in return. "Gotta go, babe. I'm being given the evil eye by some guard in an Armani suit."

"You okay?"

She laughed off Allegra's concern. "Kidding. But I do need to attend my first meeting with the prince and suck up to him."

"You're going to nail this, Zo-Zo. I have full confidence in you."

Glad someone does, Zoe thought, and not for the first time. For a woman confident in her life and her sexuality, she wasn't such a tough girl professionally. From the moment she'd accepted Allegra's offer of partnership in the advertising agency last month, she'd second-guessed her decision.

As if it wasn't bad enough that she'd lost the company's most important clients, she'd heard the office rumors, the ones that implied she'd only gotten the massive promotion because of her friendship with the boss. It pissed her off, but no way would she reveal her real reasons for staying in the background all these years despite being an equal equity partner.

Her boisterous, loud rambunctiousness may come from her brash dad, but she'd also inherited a smidgeon of her mom's circumspection when it came to private matters, and no one knew the real reason why she'd made the professional decisions she had.

But she'd been restless over the last six months, wanting to do more, wanting more responsibility. So while Allegra had been away in Palm Bay wooing their new number one client, Kai Kaluna, Zoe had tried to solidify deals with their existing clients with her usual pushy flamboyance.

And lost them in the process.

Which made it imperative she do a kick-ass job with the Kaluna Resorts campaign here and prove to everyone, including herself, she had what it took to make it in business.

"Thanks, I'll e-mail you regular updates," Zoe said. "Now go jump that hot Aussie."

"Will do." Allegra made a smoochy sound. "You know, that prince is pretty hot. Shame you can't mix business with pleasure—"

"You're breaking up, babe." Zoe rapped a manicured fingernail against the screen. "Bye."

She hit the end call button and slid the cell back into her bag.

The moment she landed this deal, she'd tell Allegra the truth. All of it.

And her plans all hinged on getting a recalcitrant prince to change his mind. Lucky her. Not.

Zoe ditched the terry robe wrapped around her body and changed into a black pinstriped business suit: fitted knee-length skirt, nipped-at-the-waist jacket, with a white silk blouse underneath. It was the most conservative outfit she owned, the one she pulled out for important business meetings, like the one she was about to attend.

She hated it. So she added more product in her hair to accentuate the razor cut, applied shimmery silver eye shadow to highlight her heavily lined eyes, and slicked a vivid crimson gloss on her lips.

She looked like a mix between corporate chic and sexpot vixen. Perfect. The first would show Prince Pedantic she was serious about her business proposal; the second would show him what he was missing out on.

Their first meeting had been disastrous. Nothing like how she'd imagined. Though it hadn't been all bad, considering she'd gotten to grope royalty.

Okay, so a hand on his chest wasn't exactly in the groping category, but it had felt mighty fine.

Crap, had she really come on to him? Not good. A professional disaster in the making. So much for redeeming herself at AW Advertising. If she kept it up, the only thing she'd prove with her first attempt at securing a mega-deal as partner would be how to make a mess of a key presentation and alienate a chunk of Europe in the process.

The part where Dominic seemed to be affected by the instantaneous attraction between them? Unexpected. As was the size of his impressive hard-on...but she wouldn't go there. If she had no scruples, she'd appeal to his male side and seduce the guy into giving her what she wanted. But Zoe had sworn she needed a new start along with her new role in the company, so she was ditching the casual dates and easy sex in favor of...what? A steady relationship for the first time in her life? A chance at falling in love? Risking her sense of identity for the sake of an emotional attachment?

She hadn't quite gotten that far in her new plans for the future, but she knew one thing: she couldn't keep doing what she'd been doing. After her last one-night stand, she'd bolted from the guy's apartment before she'd broken down in tears, saving those for the sanctity of her car, where she'd sat for an hour, bawling. That meltdown had scared the crap out of her, and she'd vowed right then to shake things up a little. Which for her meant toning down her sexuality and ditching the casual encounters.

"That's going to be fun. Not," she muttered, swiping pages on her tablet, doing a final check on her proposal. She'd put in an inordinate amount of time ensuring this proposal was the best damn thing she'd ever done. The prince had to be impressed. He just had to.

Confident all was well with her presentation, she slipped the tablet into her portfolio case.

She could do this.

But as she retraced her steps along endless corridors to the den she'd been shown as they entered, her confidence dwindled.

WANTON HEAT

Allegra had been the spokeswoman for every pitch their ad agency had ever done. Zoe had been content to do the background work, something she was damn good at. She could research and collate and brainstorm like a pro, but being front and center with a client? Not her style. As she'd already discovered the hard way.

Even the success with landing the highly lucrative Kaluna Resorts worldwide ad campaign had been done with Allegra as the boss and her along for the ride. Allegra begged to differ, but Zoe knew where her strengths lay, and schmoozing clients she'd rather slap upside the head probably wasn't one of them.

She was too outspoken, too brash to charm VIPs. Her bullshit meter was set to low, and the moment anyone started spouting crap, she called them on it. But with Allegra busy launching the new Kaluna Resort in the Whitsunday Islands, and Zoe a newly appointed partner, she'd been thrown in the deep end.

Allegra had insisted she take on the Mediterranean job, and Zoe couldn't have continued protesting without Allegra's getting suspicious. So here she was, desperate to make a good impression and secure the deal of a lifetime. And hopefully, make up for her monumental gaffe in the process.

Dominic stepped out of the den at that moment. Hot damn. The prince could fill out a suit. The designer charcoal jacket and pants fit like he'd been poured into them, while a sky-blue shirt made his eyes look impossibly indigo.

Her lungs seized a little as he locked gazes with her, his insolence both annoying and a turn-on. Then he smiled, a confident smirk that implied he could read her mind.

Man, she was so screwed.

"Ready for our meeting?" She managed to stride toward him without stumbling, clutching her portfolio tighter. "I've got a ton of information you should see."

"I doubt that," he said, his laconic drawl making her bristle. That was his intention, and she couldn't react, couldn't let him deliberately rile her when she had to nail this meeting. "But why don't you come in and give it your best shot?"

He gestured for her to pass him but didn't move, meaning she had to squeeze past him to enter the den. So His Highness didn't like to play fair? Too bad for him—she was a killer poker player and had called many a bluff.

"I guarantee you'll be impressed," she said, pausing in the doorway, ensuring their bodies were less than a few inches apart.

Heat flared in his eyes, and she resisted the urge to say "gotcha!"

If he intended to undermine her, he'd have to do better than that. She was a master flirt, one of the best, and no way would she let some high-and-mighty prince play mind games with the sole intention of rattling her.

"I already am," he said, not moving a muscle. "Very impressed."

Zoe had no idea how long they stood there, locked in a standoff, neither of them willing to back down. She could smell his expensive citrus aftershave, could see the tiniest scar beneath his right ear, could feel the heat that radiated off him. It overwhelmed her. Dominic Ricci was too arrogant, too cynical, too much.

"Good, then you'll be even more impressed when you see this." She practically shoved her portfolio in his face before slipping past him into the den.

She made it as far as a small conference table before her legs wobbled. Damn the man for having such a potent effect on her.

His business was her future. She had to remember that. Because that inner vixen she'd deliberately locked away for this entire trip? Was getting feisty, rattling her self-imposed cage to escape.

It would be immense fun to take down a smug bastard like Dominic.

"Refreshments?" He gestured at a mahogany side bar, where someone had laid out a paper-thin porcelain tea set and a mini-tray of baklava.

Her mouth watered, but she shook her head. Last thing she

needed was nuts stuck in her teeth while she tried to sway him. "No, thanks, I'd rather get started."

"Suit yourself." He sat at the head of the table, leaving her in the awkward position of having to choose a seat. It would need to be close enough to him for him to see the tablet screen, but that would be too close for comfort. Damn.

She chose the chair on his right, slid her tablet out, and set it up on its stand. It slipped slightly, courtesy of her sweaty palms, and he reached out, steadying it. Unfortunately, she'd been doing the same thing, and his hand enclosed hers. Long, elegant fingers. Broad palm. Firm grip. And heat, so much heat that seeped into her skin and zapped her arm like an injection of pheromones.

"Thanks," she said, casually slipping her hand out from under his and resisting the urge to cradle it with the other. "First, I'd like to thank you for giving AW Advertising this chance to meet with you."

"I was left no choice."

She didn't understand his bitter response, nor did she want to. She had a job to do and that was convince him that Kaluna Resort's advertising campaign was in his best interests.

Her finger swiped the tablet to bring up her first presentation slide, though she didn't need to look at the screen. She'd mentally rehearsed this a million times and could recite her spiel in her sleep.

"As I'm sure you're aware, Kai Kaluna recently hired AW Advertising to run his worldwide ad campaign for his resorts in the Whitsundays, the Caribbean, the South Pacific, Mexico, and the Mediterranean."

She brought up another slide, featuring the island of Ancora, owned by the guy sitting in front of her, eyeing her with wary disdain. "Like most of Italy, the recession has hit the Kaluna Resort on Ancora hard. Tourism is at an all-time low in this region despite the natural beauty and obvious charms."

She flicked through a few more slides, highlighting a breathtaking island she couldn't wait to explore: azure ocean, pristine beaches, secluded coves, and rocky outcrops. Ancora had captured her imagination from the first moment she'd started researching. Something about its unspoiled beauty, its inherent wildness, called to her.

"To counteract this ongoing downward trend, we propose a major worldwide campaign to attract tourists back to Ancora." She paused for emphasis. "And in turn, Osturo, considering no one can get to the other island unless they come via here."

If she'd expected a flicker of interest or a change in his dour expression, she would be disappointed. Nothing. Not even a spark.

"Kai Kaluna has set an extremely generous budget. And as you know from the e-mails the developer cc'd us both on, he needs to update the existing resort with a few minor renovations before we advertise the place to the world." She swiped to another page, showing an artist's impression of what the new, revamped Ancora resort would look like. "This is what will be the new focus of Ancora—"

"No." He stood so abruptly his chair slammed into the wall behind him.

Stunned, she stared up at him. "I beg your pardon?"

"You heard me." He towered over her, looking like a demented demon. "I said no."

"But I haven't gotten through a quarter of my presentation." Her hands fluttered helplessly between the tablet and him. "You need to see the projected figures and the spreadsheets an influx of tourists will—"

"What part of 'no' can't you understand?"

And with that, he stormed out of the room, leaving her wanting to punch something. Preferably the prince's stubborn head.

Chapter Four

Zoe took several deep calming breaths and willed her anger to fade before she did something stupid, like follow up on that impulse to punch the prince.

He'd walked out on her.

Who the hell did he think he was? A boorish, royal prick obviously used to treating people like crap, that's who.

She'd barely started her presentation, and he'd rejected it? No way would she stand for that. She'd make His Haughty Highness listen to her if she had to tie him down to do it.

An erotic image of doing just that popped into her head, and she blinked, needing to dismiss it. No time for fantasies when she had a job to do, one that didn't involve assaulting one very stubborn royal pain in the ass.

Unsure whether she should go in search of Dominic or wait until he calmed down and hopefully returned, she slid her tablet back into her portfolio and stood.

"Hope I'm not interrupting?" An elderly woman stuck her head around the door, and Zoe was instantly struck by the resemblance to

Dominic. They both had high cheekbones, a strong jaw, and those piercing blue eyes. Queen Catarina.

"Not at all," Zoe said, unsure whether to bow or grovel or kiss the woman's hand as she stepped into the den and closed the door behind her. "I'm Zoe Keaton."

She settled for holding out her hand for the queen to shake and thankfully, the older woman did just that.

"Pleased to meet you, dear. I'm Catarina."

Impressed by the queen's informality, Zoe waited until Catarina sat in Dominic's recently vacated chair before resuming her seat. "I was meeting with Dominic."

Catarina nodded. "Thought so, when I saw him storm out of here."

"He didn't like what I had to say." Catarina smiled. "He can be obtuse."

Zoe could think of other words to describe him.

"He's an astute businessman, but he's taking so long to pull this region out of its slump..." Catarina shook her head. "I sometimes wonder if he believes change on the islands will desecrate the memory of his parents."

Zoe had read about the death of Dominic's parents in a Swiss Alps avalanche three years ago, followed by the death of his fiancée in a car crash a year later. By all reports, Dominic had withdrawn from society ever since.

She didn't blame him for being a recluse—losing three people he loved in a year would devastate anyone—but she thought it was foolish for a businessman who'd studied at Oxford and spent considerable time in London's financial district to cut himself off from the running of islands he predominantly owned due to grief.

"I'm sorry for your loss," she said.

"Thank you, dear." Catarina steepled her fingers and rested her forearms on the table, pinning Zoe with a disconcerting stare. "I'll be blunt. When my son Franco died, all his land holdings on Ancora and Osturo passed to Dominic. So he owns most of the land on these islands, which are in desperate need of a financial injection. Kaluna wants to expand and advertise, but thanks to a stipulation Dominic's nonno made when the first contracts were signed, he can't move forward without Dominic's agreement." She smiled. "I'm hoping you can coerce Dominic into rethinking his rigid stance."

Disoriented by the queen's directness, Zoe responded in kind. "While I appreciate your candor, if Dominic can't be swayed by you, what makes you think I'll have more success?"

The impish gleam in Catarina's eyes made Zoe wary. "Because when people are resistant to change, it often helps to hear the harsh truth from a stranger, an impartial party."

"I'm far from impartial, considering I have an agenda in being here."

Catarina nodded. "Exactly, which is why I hope you'll listen to me."

Being given advice by Dominic's grandmother in such surreal circumstances, Zoe relaxed into her chair. "Brokering this deal is important for all of us, so whatever advice you can give me I'll take."

"It's quite simple. You need to present your offer in an environment where Dominic can't escape." Catarina's eyes sparkled with mischief, taking years off her wrinkled face.

"I'm not sure I understand?"

"You need to kidnap him."

Zoe stared at Catarina like she'd lost her mind. Kidnap Dominic? Shame her research on the queen hadn't divulged that the old woman was completely batty.

Catarina chuckled. "You had planned on touring Ancora tomorrow? Well, there's a big storm coming in. Legendary for these islands."

Zoe glanced out the window at the clear blue sky. Yep, Catarina had definitely lost her royal marbles.

"The last storm of this magnitude was forty years ago. Back then, it lasted days, so that will give you plenty of time to convince

Dominic of the wisdom of your proposal." Catarina glanced at her watch and stood. "Come. We don't have much time."

Zoe paused and racked her brain to come up with a polite way of saying "Are you out of your freaking mind?"

"I'll ensure all is in readiness at the dock, and I'll get Dominic down to the boat in an hour." Catarina's gaze flickered over her from head to foot. "That gives you plenty of time to change. The cottage we use on the island is well-stocked and has weathered many storms, so you'll be safe there."

Zoe didn't know what was worse. Being bundled off to a remote island in the middle of killer weather by a crazy queen, or acknowledging that a small part of her was actually looking forward to this. She'd thought she'd left her adventurous ways behind when she'd landed on Osturo. Maybe this new stage of her life was only just beginning?

"With all due respect, Catarina, this scheme sounds a little outlandish."

Code for "you're nuttier than a jar of peanut butter."

Catarina straightened and pinned her with an imperious gaze that certified her royal lineage. "Do you want your presentation to succeed or not?"

"Of course I do, but—"

"Then this is the way you'll succeed. Dominic is too wound up to check incoming weather, and he won't know of our collusion." Catarina's expression softened as she reached out to pat Zoe's shoulder. "Trust me, my dear. I've done an extensive background check on you. You're just the woman my grandson needs...to show him the future doesn't have to be influenced by the past."

Catarina's pause set off warning bells in Zoe's head. Surely the queen wasn't trying to matchmake? Being stranded on an island could be construed as romantic. If Zoe didn't want to kick Dominic's ass so much. But she was passing through and so far removed from the type of woman Catarina should choose for her grandson, it wasn't funny. She wasn't Italian. She wasn't nobility. She wanted something from them, and famous people hated the constant barrage of usurpers ready to take advantage of them. And lastly, she was a total stranger who could have nefarious reasons for being here. It just didn't make sense.

Unless Catarina thought her grandson needed to get laid to lighten up? Eww. Zoe wrinkled her nose at the thought.

"Are you trying to set us up?" Zoe blurted, unable to hold her tongue a second longer.

"Let's call this a mutually beneficial arrangement." Catarina's serene smile grated. "You're lively and bright and far removed from the women my grandson usually spends time with, so I'm hoping that will work in your favor to convince him of the wisdom of agreeing to advertise Ancora."

Zoe didn't buy the queen's trite speech considering the roguish twinkle in her eyes.

Catarina leaned forward like a co-conspirator. "Will you do it?"

She should say no. This was crazier than anything she'd done in the past. Kidnap a prince? What the hell was she thinking?

But she had to nail this presentation, and having a captive audience, one who couldn't escape because of a raging storm outside, sounded like an opportunity too good to pass up.

She nodded. "I'll do it."

Catarina laughed. "You won't regret it."

Zoe bit back her first response: *I already do.*

...

Dominic stomped around the glass-enclosed sunroom, resisting the urge to kick something.

Dio mio, Zoe had gotten him riled, charging into that meeting like a goddess.

Though in all fairness, the sexual awareness fizzing his blood wasn't her fault. He'd been too long without a woman, and it showed. His cock hardened every time he laid eyes on the infuriating woman. And he responded by taking his frustrations out on her.

Not good.

He shouldn't have stormed out of her presentation, no matter how pissed off he was. Would've been smarter to hear her out, then show her the door. But his grandmother had blackmailed him into allowing the representative from AW Advertising to stay for a week. See the islands. Get a feel for the campaign that would ultimately boost visitors and fill their coffers.

Now that he'd laid eyes on Zoe Keaton, he knew why. Nonna was up to her usual matchmaking tricks. And killing the proverbial two birds with one stone. Having a feisty, attractive woman trying to change his mind would achieve both of his grandmother's goals in one go. He knew she meant well, but her machinations had taken a surprising twist if she thought Zoe was his type. Or was Nonna getting cunning in her old age?

She'd failed with her last few fix-ups, women physically similar to Lilia. Maybe she'd deliberately chosen a woman he'd least likely fraternize with this time around? Knowing Nonna, she would've done a thorough background check before allowing Zoe anywhere near him, which begged the question: what was it about Zoe Keaton that had captivated his nonna as much as Zoe had him?

Why couldn't the ad agency have sent a nerdy, middle-aged man instead of a sassy twenty-something vixen? The woman was trouble. And now he'd have to apologize for being a boor.

"I hope you're going to apologize to that young lady."

Almost a direct echo of his thoughts, he turned at the sound of his grandmother's voice to find her standing in the doorway with her arms folded. A deep frown creased her brow, and she radiated disapproval. He should know. She'd been the same when he'd smashed a priceless vase at five while kicking a soccer ball inside. And at eight, when he'd trashed her prized roses while weeding in the garden. And at twenty-nine, when he'd brought Lilia home and announced her as his fiancée. *Mannaia*, had Catarina's disapproval meter shot off the scale that day. Nonna hadn't liked the cool blonde on sight. Which made her approval of Zoe all the more interesting.

Nonna had good instincts for reading people. It wasn't until Lilia's death that he understood the true meaning of treachery. Listening to Catarina's warnings might have saved him all that pain. And Nonna didn't know the half of it.

"I'll think about it," he said, sounding like a sulky brat.

She tut-tutted and entered the room. "You weren't raised to be rude."

He hadn't been raised to change the face of these islands forever, either. But he was under increasing pressure from investors, the only reason why he'd agreed to host a spokeswoman from AW Advertising here. That, and his nonna's refusal to see a cardiologist unless he agreed.

Courtesy of his grandfather, who'd brokered the first hotel deal, Kaluna had built an eco-friendly resort on Ancora and was serious about preserving the environment. An environment Dominic would do anything to protect.

Kaluna's proposed expansion and worldwide advertising campaign to draw visitors to the area may look good on paper, but the unspoiled beauty of his homeland could be lost forever.

He believed in progress. He believed in financial security for this region. What he didn't believe in was compromising his principles—his father's principles—to achieve it.

"Why are you so resistant to change, Nicci Ricci?" Great, now Nonna was pulling out the big guns, utilizing the childhood nickname only she used.

"I'm not—"

"I beg to differ." She held up a hand, the skin on the back of it almost translucent. "We're the only members of the Ricci family left, discounting your cousins Luciano and Gregoro." She made a disgusted sound. "As if those two care about our islands."

Dominic didn't blame his cousins Luc and Greg for spreading their wings beyond Europe. Both had American mothers who had married into the Ricci family, and both women had been widowed young, so it stood to reason that the boys had grown up in America. At times, Dominic envied them that freedom. They'd never had an opportunity to grow attached to the islands like he had. They'd never had the noose of responsibility gently looped around their necks in their teens like he had, by a father who adored these islands like he'd constructed them by hand. And that noose had progressively tightened since his father had died.

"Just because Luc and Greg aren't around much doesn't mean they don't care."

A fond smile creased Catarina's face. "Still defending those two louts, huh?"

"They were never half as bad as you thought." Both boys were three years older than him and according to Nonna, had consistently led him astray until they'd left Osturo at the age of thirteen. Dominic had idolized his cousins and saw them far too infrequently these days. Luc had settled in New York, Greg in Florida, a world away from here.

"They should come visit their nonna more often," she said, a hint of wistfulness mingling with the sadness in her tone. "Maybe they'll take time out of their busy schedules when I'm in a wooden box being lowered into the ground."

She made a sign of the cross, and Dominic bit back a smile. Catarina was a spry seventy-five and could reach one hundred if she paid more attention to her heart issues. But she was fond of dramatics, a by-product of watching too many soap operas on cable, her one vice.

"Maybe they can return for a holiday once the developers build high-rise resorts across the islands and tear the place apart if you have your way?"

His dry response garnered a frown from Catarina. "Allowing the Kaluna Resort to expand and advertise is savvy business." She tapped her temple. "You're a smart boy, Nicci. Do the right thing."

She paused, her serene gaze beseeching him to listen. "It's what your parents would've wanted."

A sharp pain stabbed him in the chest. That was a low blow, especially coming from Catarina. She'd been devastated losing Luc's father to cancer ten years ago, then Greg's father to complications following routine gall bladder surgery. Dominic's father had been her eldest and sole surviving son, so when he'd died in that avalanche, Catarina had clung to Dominic, the sole remaining Ricci male—and heir—still living on the island.

They'd grown closer via their sorrow, had talked many nights until dawn when insomnia had plagued them.

He wasn't a fool. He knew his impulsive engagement to Lilia had been borne of his grief. He'd needed a distraction, needed to feel happy again, and for the short time they'd been together, he had been. But it had been superficial, a brittle joy that quickly evaporated, leaving wariness and suspicion and eventually retribution in its wake.

"My parents didn't change a thing for as long as I can remember." He patted his chest. "I'm thirty-one, and not once in all those years did they condone developing these islands as a tourist mecca, let alone anything else."

Sorrow pinched Catarina's mouth, and Dominic felt instantly contrite for bringing up what must be a painful topic. "Why do you think that is?"

Confused, he shook his head. "I don't understand."

With a heavy sigh, Catarina sank onto the nearest seat, a worn chintz sofa that had once graced his playroom. "Your father was a peacemaker. He maintained the status quo in everything he did. Hated change of any kind. And while he loved these islands, he only stayed because of..."

She clamped her lips shut and darted a nervous glance out the window, like she'd said too much.

"Because of what?" Dominic prompted, feeling like he was on the verge of an important truth but reluctant to hear it for fear it would change everything.

"Forget I said anything—"

"Nonna, tell me."

She inhaled sharply, worry lines fanning from the corners of her mouth. "Because of you," she said, so softly it almost came out a whisper. "Your mother wanted to live on the mainland. Rome. Tuscany. Anywhere but here." She sniffed. "But my Franco wouldn't hear of it. He wanted his son to have a chance to know his heritage. To have the choice to know these islands like he did, if that's what you wanted."

A lone tear seeped from the corner of her eye and trickled down her cheek, but it didn't dampen the determination in her defiant stare. "Franco didn't change anything, because he loved this place." She pointed at him. "But he loved something else more. You."

That pain earlier? Blossomed into a diffuse ache that pressed against Dominic's chest like he was having a heart attack. All this time, he'd assumed his father had been a homebody because he loved these islands so much. But Dominic had been the one tying his dad to this place. He'd been the one holding his parents back from moving away.

What he'd just learned? Cemented his resolve. If his father had gone to such great lengths to give him the opportunity to love these islands, the least Dom could do was preserve them in honor of his father's memory.

"I didn't know," he said, crossing the room to sit beside her and grasp her hand. "You should've told me."

"I didn't see the point 'til now." She squeezed his hand in return. "You need to make your own decisions, Nicci. Based on what *you* want, not what you think your father would've wanted."

Nonna was right. But couldn't she see what she'd told him made him feel more indebted to his father than ever?

There was no way he could approve the Kaluna Resort worldwide ad campaign, now more than ever. But he'd promised Catarina to consider what they had to offer, and she could out-stubborn him, so unless he went through with this farcical charade of listening to the rest of Zoe's pitch, she'd make his life hell.

"You should take Zoe to Ancora. Let her finish her proposal. Then make an objective decision."

Great, just what he needed, to take that upstart to his favorite place in the world. He knew she'd need to see it at some stage but had planned to fob her off onto a guide. But now he realized he'd need to hear the rest of her ideas to ensure he could refuse with a clean slate.

The e-mails the developer had sent hadn't inspired him with confidence, so he was glad he now had a PI digging into Kai Kaluna's business plans. With a little luck, he'd get some concrete evidence to back up his stance in ultimately refusing Zoe Keaton.

Catarina continued. "If you hear her pitch on the island, see what she has planned firsthand, maybe you'll be more open-minded when it comes to moving ahead?"

As if. The part where an instant image of Zoe on Ancora in a miniscule caramel bikini, the same color as her eyes, popped into his head? Not helping.

She better not pack a frigging bathing suit.

"Okay, I'll take her over later."

He didn't understand Catarina's triumphant grin. "Good boy. You should head down to the docks, clear your head, make sure the boat's ready."

"Maybe I should apologize to Zoe first?"

He'd acted like a prize ass, and knowing the confident woman, she probably wouldn't let him forget it.

"I'll find her and let her know what you intend to do. Probably best you give her some time to forgive your rudeness?"

Dominic managed a wry grin as he kissed his grandmother on the cheek. "How did you get so wise?"

"When you live through as many long, hot Osturo summers as I have, you get to know a thing or two." She patted his cheek. "Now go get organized for your trip to Ancora."

Dominic needed no encouragement to head to his favorite place in the world. Having Zoe along for the ride? Challenging at best. At worst? The two of them alone at the secluded royal enclave on the island...sparring and annoying each other and causing some serious fireworks.

Damn it, he didn't want to be attracted to her. She was only here for one thing: to get the go-ahead on her proposed ad campaign. One of the many countless people over the years who wanted something from him. He should be used to it. He'd honed his instincts to read people over the years, unsurprised to discover most who hung around him did it only because they had an agenda.

So what was it about Zoe that crept under his guard a little?

He knew she was only here for business, so why couldn't he stop thinking about mixing it with pleasure?

He could take the heat, could take whatever she dished out.

But was she ready to accept the consequences of playing with fire?

Chapter Five

Zoe had a bad feeling about this.

Agreeing to Catarina's madcap scheme to kidnap Dominic had sounded crazy at the time, but now that she was on the boat, lying in wait for the unsuspecting prince, it seemed a thousand times nuttier.

Luckily, her dad had been an accomplished sailor, so she knew how to handle a boat courtesy of their frequent trips to San Diego. While the prince's seemed sleeker and faster than anything she'd operated before, she'd taken a crash course with the captain, who was now firmly ensconced in the harbor cafeteria, a small five-table room that catered to weary travelers in need of quick sustenance. Catarina had rung ahead and advised they didn't need his services for this trip. She'd thought of everything.

Except one thing.

Big, bad, brave Zoe was having a distinct case of cold feet. She eyed her overnight bag tucked under a highly polished mahogany table in the hold below. If she grabbed it now, she'd still have time to make a run for it...

A footfall sounded on the deck, and she peeked out from her hiding spot starboard.

Dominic.

He stood aft, silhouetted against the darkening sky, staring into the distance. He'd changed out of his suit and now wore knee-length khaki shorts, a white polo shirt, and docksiders. The way that polo molded to his torso and the shorts to his butt...maybe spiriting him away to a secluded island wasn't so crazy after all.

Thankfully, she'd had the foresight to loosen the moorings, so all she had to do was slip the last rope off. Barefoot, she silently padded to the bow, casting nervous glances over her shoulder. She'd lost sight of Dominic now so had to work fast. She leaned over, unhooked the last rope, and sidled backward. Her heart pounded in her ears as she slipped behind the controls. Her hands shook as she followed the start-up routine the captain had shown her, and she blinked sweat out of her eyes.

This was categorically the craziest thing she'd ever done. The engine started with a roar the first time, and she let out an exultant whoop. Footsteps thundered behind her, the sound of loud cursing in Italian reaching her ears a second before Dominic entered the driver's cabin.

"What the fuck are you doing?"

"Who would've thought royalty swears like a sailor?" With a jaunty salute, she maneuvered the boat and it shot off, earning another round of vociferous swearing from Dominic.

"Are you insane?" He sat next to her, alternating between staring at her in shock and absolute terror as she handled the controls like a pro. "Can you even operate this thing?"

"With my eyes closed." She demonstrated by doing just that, and the boat jolted a little.

"Move over."

She bristled at his command. "You didn't say please." It made more sense for him to man the controls, but she wouldn't put up with his arrogance. Even if the water's reflection in his mesmerizing eyes made them impossibly bluer.

"Move, or I'll call the coast guard and have you arrested for stealing."

"Don't forget kidnapping." She snapped her fingers. "Because that's what I've done, you know. Kidnapped you."

"I thought you were yet another leech out for whatever you can get from me, but isn't this taking things to extremes?" He glowered. "Why are you doing this?"

"You'll find out when we get to Ancora." She pointed at the radar. "That's where we're going, by the way, in case you were wondering."

"You're not supposed to tell your captive what you have planned." His surliness eased as the corners of his mouth curved into a semi-smile. "Pity, though."

Startled by his abrupt change in mood, she said, "What's a pity?"

"For a moment, I thought you might've kidnapped me so you could have your wicked way with me."

"You wish," she muttered, annoyed by heat flushing her cheeks in a dead giveaway of exactly how wicked she'd like to get with the hot prince.

"I wish for a lot of things, *cara*." He leaned closer, and her fingers clenched the steering wheel.

"Like world peace?" She stared straight ahead, pretending not to notice his proximity. Damn, she could smell him again, a tantalizing mix of sea air and sexy male.

"Like a better life for the people on these islands. Like financial security for the region." His breath fanned her ear. "Like a woman to be stranded on Ancora with..."

Oh, boy. Looked like His Highness was about to get his wish.

"To be my sex slave," he added, and this time her hands did slip off the wheel.

"Shit," she muttered, and he laughed.

This time, when he said move over, she obeyed, changing seats with him in a hurry.

"So how about it?"

He cast her a playful look she couldn't fathom, and while Zoe would have liked nothing better than to flirt back, she had to convince this moody man that her ad campaign was a winner. With a bit of luck, she could do that this afternoon, and they might have time to play, waiting out the storm before heading back to Osturo. Sounded like a plan.

"Don't go getting any ideas," she said, tilting her nose in the air. "This kidnapping is for business purposes only. I need you to hear me out and not behave like a big baby by walking out, so here we are."

He chuckled at her haughtiness. "You could've just asked. I was planning on taking you to Ancora this afternoon anyway." His smile faded. "After I apologized, that is."

Who knew? His Haughtiness did have a soul.

"I'm listening," she said, finally relaxing into her seat now that she knew he wasn't super pissed at her for kidnapping him, and he wasn't going to throw her overboard.

"I'm sorry for walking out on you," he said, sounding suitably sincere. "It was unprofessional."

"And childish," she said, unable to resist baiting him a little. "And incredibly sulky. Bet you were the kid who threw a tantrum when the silver spoon was ripped from his mouth—"

"Shut up." He took his eyes off the water for a moment to stare at her lips, and she could've sworn her gloss evaporated clear off. "You should put that mouth to better use."

Stunned by his innuendo, Zoe didn't say a word.

He smirked at her speechlessness and refocused on the water. "This kidnapping caper isn't so bad after all."

She begged to differ.

...

WANTON HEAT

. . .

As the boat cut through the water toward Ancora, Dominic felt some of the residual tension he wore like a coat these days dissipate.

When was the last time he'd headed out here, let alone taken the boat for a spin?

It used to be one of his favorite relaxation methods, to leave everything behind and spend a few days in solitude. If the rooftop conservatory in the castle had been his go-to place as a kid, Ancora assumed that honor when he hit his teens. He didn't bring many people out here, and certainly not any of his dates. It spoke volumes that Lilia hadn't seen the island either. She hadn't been interested, spending most of her time jetting from Rome to Milan to Venice, overseeing the fashion buyers for her parents' couture house. When they caught up, it was usually in Rome, where he indulged her passion for dining in fine restaurants, theater, and shopping. Sadly that passion hadn't extended to all areas of her life.

He hadn't minded at the time, content to lose himself in a relationship that brought stability and warmth to his life at a time he needed it most. Lilia's enthusiasm had thawed his frozen heart following his parents' death. She'd resuscitated him. Only to plunge him back into despair when she died a year later in a horrific head-on collision. While in the car of a developer who wasn't averse to trying any tactic to get him to sell Osturo land, apparently.

Dominic never knew if Lilia had been unfaithful or if she was just plain greedy, hell-bent on getting him to agree to anything, including pillage the island he called home. But he'd seen the evidence of her treachery when he'd cleared out his things from her apartment in Rome and had discovered irrefutable proof—copies of soil reports, zoning permits, and all the land deeds he owned on Osturo—that his trust had been violated.

Never again.

Mulling that awful time made him pull out his cell to check his e-mails. With a little luck he'd have some more info from the PI. Info he could use to help send his kidnapper back to the mainland once and for all.

He quickly scrolled through his in-box. Nada from the investigator. So he fired off another e-mail asking to be kept informed of any developments ASAP before sliding the phone back into his pocket.

He needed to be prepared. Needed to prevent being taken for a fool again.

He'd shut himself off from everyone the last few years. He heard the rumors: distraught prince loses parents and fiancée, becomes a heartbroken recluse who was letting his royal municipality rot.

They couldn't be more wrong.

He'd grieved for his parents, had dealt with Lilia's betrayal and death, but his heart was far from broken. He'd just learned to protect it better. As for letting Osturo and Ancora rot, there was a difference between protecting what was his, bestowed upon him by his father, and carving it up for the almighty euro.

"Are we nearly there yet?"

He glanced at the woman by his side, struck anew by her beauty. Zoe had swapped her pin-striped suit for a sassy sunflower-yellow summer dress with thin straps, a fitted bodice that outlined her generous breasts to perfection, and a flirty skirt that ended at her knees.

She looked bright and sunny and delectable. And in that moment, it hit him: how long since he'd enjoyed the pleasure of a woman, of being with a woman, for no other reason than to flirt and seduce.

He would love to do both with this intriguing woman. But he couldn't. She wanted something from him, something he couldn't give.

He'd hear her out, then send her on her way. After a little harmless flirtation...

"Eager to get me alone?" He touched her hand, a fingertip brushing her knuckle in a feather-light caress that elicited a slight tremor. Oh, yeah, she was just as aware of him physically as he was of her. He bet they'd be combustible together. Shame he'd never find out.

"Eager to have your full attention," she said, sliding her hand away to clasp it with the other in her lap.

"You already have that." His lips eased into a smile, and it felt good. He didn't smile much these days. Then he realized he was grinning like a fool at the enemy, and he clamped his lips tight.

She rolled her eyes. "For my presentation."

"Thanks for the clarification," he said, expressing silent gratitude to the weather gods when a gust of wind ruffled the hem of her skirt, flipping it to mid-thigh.

"I'll make you listen to me this time if it kills me," she muttered, smoothing her skirt. "Hopefully you'll be less grumpy and more cheerful on Ancora."

"Do I look like I'm grumpy?" He winked, enjoying the suspicious glare she shot him. Meant he had her off-kilter. Good. Because that's the way he'd been feeling ever since he met her prowling the castle grounds. "Considering you kidnapped me, I'd say I'm handling the situation admirably."

"Yeah, you're a real prince," she said, the corners of her lush mouth twitching.

"You know that's an empty title, right?" He jerked a thumb over his shoulder in the direction of the hold. "I bet you've got a ton of research notes on me in that bag of yours."

"Most people in the twenty-first century research on the *Internet*," she said. "You know, that online thing that has search engines designed to find out every nitty-gritty detail about people's lives."

He grinned at her sarcasm. "Damn, I knew I was doing something wrong, using those coconut-and-string phones."

She tilted her head, studying him. "What did you mean, being the prince is an empty title?"

"Guess your trusty Internet didn't tell you everything."

"Just tell me already," she said, her audible exasperation tempered with curiosity.

"Okay." He steered the boat by rote, though a quick glance at the radar showed a fast-moving front heading their way. He'd have to make their tour of the island quick. "But to answer your first question, we're about ten minutes away from Ancora."

She shot an anxious glance over her shoulder, where storm clouds were rolling in behind them.

"Don't worry. We'll be on the island before the storm hits." He gestured at the darkening sky. "We get these summer storms all the time. They blow in and out, over before you know it."

By the slight frown creasing her brow, she didn't believe him. So he distracted her with a topic most people found infinitely interesting. "The world seems fascinated by royalty, but on our islands? The Ricci family is nothing more than a living part of history."

Interest sparked her eyes, lighting the caramel flecks in a sea of chocolate brown. "So you just use the prince title to win friends and influence poor unsuspecting women?"

He snorted. "The kinds of women wooed by a title aren't worth pursuing."

"Voice of experience?"

"Something like that." He spotted land in the distance, and a jolt of familiar excitement made him clench the wheel. Why hadn't he done this sooner? Returning to Ancora never failed to make everything seem better. "So do you want to hear our history or not?"

"I guess."

She sounded like a sulky child as she continued to glance over her shoulder at the storm clouds chasing them.

"There are many principalities throughout Europe with royalty dating back centuries. Titles passed down through generations. My family owns land on Osturo and Ancora but only because the deeds were purchased by my great-grandfather. So technically, we're responsible for the financial operations. But in modern times? The actual crown and title mean little, other than as a way to impress gullible females." He threw that last bit in to get a rise out of her, and it worked.

"So you do use it as a pickup line?"

"Some women are shallow." He shrugged. "What's a guy to do?"

"Sleep his way through countless swooning females?"

"Yeah, right," he muttered, wishing Zoe hadn't mentioned anything remotely to do with sex. Because now that's what he was thinking about. With her.

"Yeah, like you've ever been through a drought," she said, jabbing him in the arm with her elbow. "Bet you've got a harem tucked away in the castle dungeons."

"That's one hell of an imagination." And he wondered how far it extended. "What about you? How many boyfriends are you fending off at the moment?"

Real subtle, Ricci. Not.

The thought was closely followed by *why the hell do you care?*

She'd be gone ASAP if he had his way. Yet another person who wanted a piece of him, the type of person he'd usually despise. He had to stop thinking about her as a desirable woman he'd soon be alone with on his favorite island.

"Single and loving it," she said, sounding anything but. He heard the wistfulness underlying her tone, as if she wanted something more. He knew the feeling.

"Not a relationship person?"

"Not really." She turned away to stare out the opposite side of the boat, effectively shutting him out.

"Surprising." He could see the east side of the island now, and his heartbeat quickened. "Most women want marriage and kids and a happily ever after."

"I'm not most women," she said, her audible defiance much more encouraging than her sadness of a moment ago.

"Lucky me."

She swiveled back to face him, and the flicker of sadness in her eyes shocked him. Why was she so despondent? And who had made her like that? It shouldn't bother him, seeing her so vulnerable, but it did. And it made him like her all the more when every logical cell in his body screamed he should keep his distance from her.

"You're a walking, talking contradiction," she said, making it sound like he'd dunked all the local sea life in a vat of acid. "I don't like game-playing. It's a waste of time. So the flirting? You either follow through, or shut the hell up."

He stared at her, gobsmacked. He'd never met anyone so outspoken, without a care for what he'd think. It was refreshing. And a major turn-on.

"Describe the follow through." He threw it out there as a challenge, wanting her to articulate exactly what sex between them would entail.

She glared at him through narrowed eyes. "Still game-playing, I see, which means you need to shut up."

He laughed, his first genuine belly laugh in years. "Okay, I'll be quiet 'til we get to the island. But *cara*?" He trailed a fingertip down her thigh, savoring the shiver of awareness that made her wrap her arms around her middle. "When we arrive on Ancora? All bets are off."

Chapter Six

Zoe didn't know what terrified her more.

The murky darkness of the storm clouds chasing them or the increasing compulsion to jump Dominic.

Damn the man. He was too sexy for his own good. And hers.

Why the hell couldn't he have been the gardener or the boat captain or the stable boy, so she could've had wild sex without the consequences?

Because there would be consequences for sleeping with the prince, she had no doubt.

Not that he'd follow through. She knew what he was doing, trying to undermine her before she could finish her presentation. Well, let him keep trying. He was dealing with the wrong woman if he thought his charm would rattle her. She could flirt like a pro. Besides, even if they both lost their minds and ended up having sex, he didn't have his professional reputation on the line, or plans for a very different future.

She had to convince him to agree to Kaluna's tourism-boosting plans. Having hot island sex would undermine her pitch. And her.

Because even though she didn't want to admit the truth, Dominic Ricci appealed to her on a deeper level than just physical.

And it scared the hell out of her.

She'd vowed to change her lifestyle. Losing the company's most valuable clients, losing her shit when she bawled after her last one-night stand, ensured she had to do things differently. So how did craving casual sex with a prince she'd just met fit in with her new plans? It didn't. But it didn't stop her from wanting to do just that.

She hadn't liked him grumpy and aloof. She liked his new humorous, flirty side even less. It disarmed her. And really made her want to tear her clothes off, straddle him, and not clamber off for a week.

"What do you think?"

She jumped at the sound of his voice. What did she think? Sex with him was a monumentally bad idea, but she wanted it regardless.

She opened her eyes and focused on the most beautiful stretch of beach she'd ever seen. A secluded alcove, sheltered on all sides by towering cliff faces, with a lone jetty jutting out in the most sheltered part.

"It's beautiful," she said, her pulse picking up tempo now they'd arrived.

"Thank you."

The emotion in his voice, the genuine gratitude, surprised her, and she turned to face him. What she saw then surprised her even more. The glimmer of tears in his eyes.

Fuck.

"This place is special to me," he said, cutting the engine. He stood and busied himself with mooring, effectively buying some time to recompose himself.

Good, because she could do with a few moments herself. She'd never seen a guy cry. Discounting the football-crazed moron she'd dated her first year in college who'd actually sniveled when his team missed out on the Super Bowl by a touchdown.

But to see a guy show genuine emotion? It choked her up. And if this storm was as bad as Catarina predicted, she'd be stranded here with him for at least two days.

Man, she was in so much trouble.

She grabbed her bag from the hold, wishing she'd never agreed to this crazy-ass scheme. If she were back on Osturo, she could've regrouped in her room, planning her next line of attack to convince Dominic her proposal was exactly what the prince ordered. But here? With those scary-looking clouds increasingly ominous and the gusty wind picking up, she'd have no option but to wait it out with him in the cottage Catarina had mentioned.

And that's the moment she realized she'd forgotten to ask the all-important question.

How many bedrooms did the cottage have?

She'd been so flabbergasted by Catarina's fiendish idea initially, and later been busy perpetrating it with little time, that she'd omitted the important stuff. Logically, any royal abode would have a squillion rooms, but Ancora was a tiny, remote island. Would the Ricci cottage be just that? A small one-room place?

"Ready to come ashore?" Dominic stood on the jetty, holding his hand out to her.

Thankfully, his tears had disappeared, but the soft expression in his eyes told her how much this place meant to him. Great. Wait until she ruined his sentimental journey by bombarding him with her pitch.

"Yeah, thanks." She slung her overnight bag higher on her shoulder and placed her other hand in his.

A little shiver of excitement shot through her as his fingers curled over hers, his palm warm and solid as he gave a little tug. A tug that was way too forceful as she stepped onto the dock. A tug that landed her flush against his chest. The excitement of a moment ago? Ratcheted up fast.

"Watch your step," he said, with a low chuckle.

"You did that on purpose." She placed her palms on his chest, his broad, bronzed, beautiful chest, and shoved, instantly regretting when he released her.

"So what if I did?" His lips curved into a lazy smile. "What are you going to do about it?"

She glared at him, desperately trying to muster indignation. But with him standing on the dock, silhouetted against a darkening sky with a towering cliff behind him, his eyes radiating blue fire, she couldn't.

If she didn't get this ad campaign proposal signed off on ASAP, she wouldn't be responsible for her actions. The new her had a clear goal in mind. The old her had sex with a prince in mind. The two were poles apart.

"What I'm going to do is make sure you listen to what I have to say." She squared her shoulders, which drew his gaze to her breasts. Damn it. "Besides, those clouds are getting angrier by the minute. Let's find shelter."

"I get it." He reached for her bag, and she considered resisting for a second before handing it over. No point pissing him off by ignoring his chivalry. "You're eager to get me alone in the cozy cottage."

Cozy? Yikes. "How cozy are we talking?"

"What do you mean?"

Here went nothing. "How many bedrooms does it have?"

He halted and she was forced to do the same. "Why? Not like we're going to be staying here overnight." He pointed skyward. "This'll blow over, and we'll be back on Osturo tonight."

This was her moment to come clean. To tell him the truth about her dastardly plan.

But was it her fault if he couldn't read his region's weather patterns after all these years? If he loved this place so much, why didn't he know this was no ordinary storm?

Conscience appeased—yeah, she had to keep telling herself that—she shrugged. "Guess I'm still a tad jet-lagged, so I thought I could take a nap this afternoon."

His eyes narrowed, as if he didn't buy her excuse for a second. "You don't seem like the napping type."

She wasn't, but now she'd headed down a one-way road to Fibsville, she had to go on with it. "You're very good at judging people. Maybe I am the *napping type*."

"And you're very good at deflection." His astute gaze never left hers. "You're up to something."

"Yeah, trying to get you alone in a single-bedroom cottage." She rolled her eyes. "And you didn't answer my question."

Tiny lines fanned out from the corners of his eyes as he laughed. "Does it matter? One bedroom or ten, the doors don't have locks, so I can disturb your nap any time I like."

This time, the shiver that racked her body was pure, unadulterated need.

"Only if you want your crown jewels crushed," she said, flouncing ahead of him on the rocky path leading upward and curving around the cliff face.

"I think you're mistaking crushing for caressing," he called after her, his mocking laughter making her want to join in.

A pox on him for being so goddamn irresistible.

Being stranded on an island with a sexy prince for longer than a day? Wasn't just a dumbass idea. With him determined to undermine her by constantly flirting, her grand plan had just entered certifiable territory.

...

As they neared the cottage, Dominic cast a quick glance at the sky.

He'd lived through a few big storms in this area over the years. It was why the cottage was always fully stocked for any eventuality with the unpredictable weather. It didn't usually bother him. He liked storms. The louder the thunder, the gustier the wind, the more he loved it. Loved sitting inside the cottage with its 360-degree views of the island, watching lightning light up the sky.

Not this time.

It had been too long since he'd been out here, and he'd made an error in judgment. By the looks of those clouds and the strength of the wind, this wasn't one of the "blow over in an afternoon" storms he'd told Zoe about.

Uh-uh. This was the kind to strand them indoors for days.

Fuck.

He wouldn't be able to keep his hands off her.

And that was a disaster waiting to happen.

It didn't sit well with him, knowing she was wasting her time with whatever she presented, but he wanted to sleep with her regardless. Only a complete bastard would do that. Unless she was agreeable for a little recreational sex to blow off steam?

Except for one salient fact: she seemed to not want him. Once he'd gotten past his initial annoyance at being kidnapped, he'd turned on the charm. Initially to rattle her, later because he enjoyed getting a rise out of her. While her heated gaze indicated a response, she hadn't fired back with the flirty quips he'd expected. Was he so starved for female attention lately that he'd misread the signals?

The few times she had responded with a fiery barb had turned him on. Big-time. He loved an intelligent woman, the ability to create sparks with words. Intellectual foreplay was incredibly stimulating before sex. Sex he couldn't stop thinking about whenever he was around Zoe Keaton, apparently, despite her being off-limits if he wanted to do this right.

He should revert to the asshole he'd been when she first arrived. His usual suspicious, aloof self. Otherwise he was in grave danger of saying to hell with his principles and seducing her regardless.

"Hope you packed your PJs," he said, gesturing to the giant bag she clutched tight as they neared the cottage. "We could be stuck here overnight."

"Not a problem." She snuck him a sideways glance. "I go commando."

He stumbled, and she laughed. "You're too easy."

"I could be for you."

He threw it out there, expecting an instant rebuttal or for her to withdraw like she had on the boat. Instead, she raised an eyebrow and fixed him with a challenging stare he had no hope of interpreting.

"News flash, Your Highness." She jabbed a finger in his direction. "You couldn't handle me."

"Want to make a bet?"

She ignored him and preceded him along the path. "I'm the enemy, remember? And *yet another leech* wanting something from you, apparently. So quit trying to charm the pants off me, and let's get inside before Mother Nature goes crazy."

"Is it working?"

She glanced over her shoulder and caught him staring at her ass. "What?"

"Is my charm working?" He deliberately stared at her legs. "Are your pants on or off?"

He could've sworn she muttered, "That's for me to know and for you to find out," before she snorted and kept walking.

With the wind whipping her lemon sundress around her thighs, and her shapely calves on full display, Dominic was heavily leaning toward the seduction option.

He shouldn't. He couldn't.

But he couldn't dislodge the persistent thought that once Zoe presented her proposal, maybe it wouldn't hurt to discover whether his charm had succeeded or not.

Chapter Seven

They reached the cottage as the first roll of thunder rumbled across the murky sky. Zoe barely had time to admire the sandstone exterior before Dominic had unlocked the door and bundled her inside.

"What's the hurry?"

"You'll see," he said, making a quick, perfunctory check of the window locks, his grim determination scaring her a little.

How bad was this storm going to be?

About ten seconds later, she had her answer. A massive zigzag of lightning lit up the sky, ending in a loud crack that made her jump.

"That was close," he said, gesturing her closer to the front window. "Come look."

Was he nuts? Back home, she'd have the curtains drawn and would be hiding inside a closet with a storm this bad. She'd never liked thunder, had never forgotten her dad telling her it was God's way of showing how angry he was with kids who didn't behave. Thunder had petrified her as a kid, and having her tree house struck by lightning and demolished as a result hadn't helped.

"I'm fine over here," she said, not moving from the doorway to a spacious lounge complete with ruby suede sofas, a handmade coffee table, and thick, plush ebony rugs. The furniture contrasted perfectly with the ivory sandstone floor and walls. Fire and ice. Beautiful.

"You're scared?" He sounded incredulous, and it made her bristle.

"Don't be stupid. I just don't like standing in front of a window when I could be struck dead by a stray bolt of lightning."

"I'll protect you." He strode across the room, stopping two feet away when she tried to ward him off with a hand that embarrassingly shook. "Shit, you're seriously scared."

"Who knew, the prince is an Einstein, too," she said, trying to cross her arms. But she was too late, and he snatched her hand and rubbed it between his.

"You can wait this out in the bedroom if you're freaked. Close the blinds. But it might take a while."

Touched by his thoughtfulness when she didn't want to be, she responded, "You'd do anything to get me into the bedroom."

The tension pinching his mouth eased. "Yeah, that's me. So powerful I can control the weather."

"As well as your minions, don't forget them."

His hands slowed, and she realized the trembling from fear of the storm had been replaced by trembling of a different kind—a deep-seated yearning making her quiver with how much she wanted him.

"I told you, don't get hung up on the prince title."

"So you're just a mere mortal male beneath all that?" She eased her hand out of his and gestured at his clothes. Wishing she hadn't when the memory of how he looked without them popped into her head. Though next time if she had him semi-naked, she'd definitely whip off that towel.

"Care to find out?" He took a step closer, and her heart flip-flopped.

She couldn't do this. Couldn't have sex with the one guy she needed on board to make amends for what she'd done to Allegra and their company.

Tell that to her unruly hormones, who right at this very second were urging her to do unthinkably dirty things with the exceptionally hot guy within touching distance.

"I don't like you," she said, desperate for a diversion and blurting the first thing that popped into her head.

If she'd expected it to deter him, it didn't.

He grinned, the predatory, smug grin of a guy who knew what he wanted and was looking straight at it.

"The feeling's mutual, *cara*, but liking isn't essential for what I have in mind."

She shouldn't ask him; she really shouldn't. But she couldn't resist. "And what's that?"

"You really want to know?" He took another step closer, and this time, less than an inch separated their bodies. "Because once I tell you, there will be no turning back."

Back off now, screamed her conscience.

To hell with it, murmured her inner bad girl.

"Maybe you're all talk? Maybe you're trying to distract me so I botch my presentation? Maybe you're just toying with me in some warped game you play with all your women—"

His mouth crushed hers. Silencing her. Tormenting her. He backed her up against the nearest wall. Sandstone dug into her back. She didn't care.

He ravished her mouth and ground his pelvis against her. She responded by nipping his tongue and hooking a leg around his waist.

They had too many clothes on.

A thought apparently shared by the prince as his hand slid beneath her skirt and ripped her panties off.

She whimpered. He deepened the kiss until she could barely breathe.

His fingertips grazed her thighs, her hips, her ass. Light, feathery touches that pebbled her skin and made her shiver with want.

She wriggled against him, desperate for him to touch her where she throbbed. But His Highness seemed intent on teasing her, because he eased the pressure against her mouth, making her whimper.

He grazed her lips repeatedly, maddeningly soft, incredibly sensual. And all the while, his fingertips maintained their leisurely exploration beneath her skirt, driving her wild with the urge to rip everything off and ride him into oblivion.

When his fingers scraped the tender skin on the inside of her thigh, she moaned so loud it echoed all the way down to her soul.

And that's when Dominic sensed her urgency. His lips slammed against hers. Devouring her mouth. Driving her insane with the relentless craving to have him inside her. Now.

Zoe knew she should stop this madness. She really should. But then he touched her clit, a slow, deliberate swipe that had her insides clenching. She really needed to be clenching around him.

She tried to insinuate her hands between their bodies, but he wouldn't let her, maintaining his sensual assault on her mouth while his thumb circled her clit.

Her orgasm built too quickly, and she tried to squirm away. It was too fast, too intense, too much. She was out of control, on a one-way trip to hedonistic heaven, without any fricking clue of how to come back.

He slid a finger inside her in response. Another. Then another. Stretching her. Filling her. Pumping into her while his thumb picked up the pace.

The pleasure built. Her muscles tightened. And then she shattered, screaming into his mouth as she came.

She was only vaguely aware of the unzipping and the tearing of foil. But her awareness improved when he gripped her ass, hoisted her up, and slid into her.

Jeez, he was big. Seriously big. Filling her so deeply, so completely, to the point of pain. Then he moved, sliding slowly out and in again, and that fleeting pain was replaced by exquisite, mind-numbing pleasure.

He nuzzled the tender skin beneath her ear. She bit his shoulder.

He nipped her earlobe. She licked beneath his jaw.

He thrust into her so deep, she almost saw stars. She scoured his back so hard he groaned, and she wasn't sure if it was in a good way.

When he changed the angle of his pelvis, driving into her deeper than she ever thought possible, she had an epiphany. Sex before Dominic? Merely a prelude to the real thing.

This was rough and ready and oh so wild.

Her second orgasm slammed into her unexpectedly but was just as cataclysmic as the first. He tensed a second later before he came, his moan drowned out by a crash of thunder.

Zoe had no idea how long they stood there, him buried inside her, her legs cramping, the rough-hewn wall digging into her back, the wind howling outside, and the lightning illuminating the room.

She didn't care. For as long as she focused on the sensational sex they'd just had, she could drown out the insistent thoughts, most of them centered on "what the fuck have you just done?"

Chapter Eight

Dominic had no idea what the hell had just happened.

One minute he'd been deliberately baiting Zoe to see how far he could go to rattle her, the next he'd shoved her up against the wall and had mind-blowing sex. In silence. No murmured endearments, no sexy whispers. He'd taken her. Hard and fast and rough.

Merda. Worse than shit. She must think he was some kind of animal.

He eased out of her and waited until her legs hit the floor before releasing her. He couldn't even look her in the eye.

"I'll be back in a second," he said, heading to the bathroom to take care of business. All the while chastising himself for being a heartless Neanderthal.

He took his time. Splashed water on his face. Tried to ignore the devastating guilt in his eyes as he stared in the mirror.

How on earth could he face this woman for business now?

That mental pep talk on the boat? The one where he knew it'd be wrong to have sex with her when he had no intention of even considering her proposal? When he'd accused her of being exactly like the rest of the suck-ups in his life? Obliterated the moment he kissed her.

Yeah, he was a heartless bastard. He should apologize, then keep his distance until they were done on the island and could go their separate ways.

So why was he eager to find her again? And eager for more. So much more.

When he returned to the lounge, she was nowhere to be found, and for an insane moment he wondered if she'd chosen to brave the storm rather than face him. Then he heard a clang in the kitchen and he headed that way, surprised to find her rummaging in the pantry. She was bent over, checking out the bottom shelves, her sexy ass in the air. Covered by that little yellow sundress only, because he'd shredded her panties.

His cock hardened immediately. What he wouldn't give to cross the kitchen in three strides, flip that skirt up, and take her from behind.

"I want pancakes, and I can't find the flour," she said, shoving canisters aside. "Are you going to help or stand there staring at my ass all day?"

The fact that she'd made a joke encouraged him. So she wasn't mad at his he-man act. But he still had no idea how to respond. Should he apologize? Laugh it off? Grovel?

"Did I mention my blood sugar goes haywire when I'm hungry, and I go a little nuts?" She finally straightened and whirled to face him, her gaze zeroing in on the obvious bulge in his shorts. "While I appreciate the sentiment and could go for round two, sex makes me ravenous, and I need to eat now."

Startled by her brazenness, he stepped into the kitchen and headed for the stove, where he busied himself finding the right size pan. "There's premade pancake mix in a stone canister on the top shelf. Long-life milk on the bottom shelf."

"Thanks."

WANTON HEAT

When she turned away and wasn't watching him with wide-eyed wariness, he said, "I'm sorry about before. I shouldn't have—"

"You're apologizing for the sex?" She whirled on him, radiating indignation. "Don't do that, okay? It was phenomenal." Her shoulders slumped. "And wrong on so many levels I can't begin to articulate. But it's done. We both enjoyed it. At least, I did, and I'm assuming you did, too?"

He heard her hint of vulnerability, and it made him want to sweep her into his arms and hold her. He settled for banging the pan on the stove instead. "It has been a long time for me, so yes, the sex was amazing."

She puffed up like an outraged bullfrog. "So anyone would've done? Is that what you're saying?"

"No, of course not." Shit, he was making a mess of this. "You were...incredible," he finished lamely, not wanting to say she was the best sex he'd ever had. For the simple fact of how responsive and uninhibited she'd been.

She hadn't wanted the lights on or thousand-thread-count sheets. She hadn't wanted thirty minutes of dictated foreplay or nonstop compliments. She'd matched him, clawing and writhing and just being in the moment.

It had been fucking unbelievable.

Wildly erotic and he'd be hard for a week just remembering every detail: the sounds she made, the way she bit him, how she wanted him all the way.

"I can live with incredible," she said, a small, smug smile curving her kiss-ravaged lips. "But as much as I'd like to stand here and discuss your prowess, I need pancakes. Stat."

He could handle cooking pancakes. What he couldn't handle was the relentless urge to hoist her onto the kitchen bench and do her again.

"You mix, I'll fry," he said, firing up the stove and spraying the pan with oil. He needed to keep busy. Needed to focus on something other than sex.

He succeeded for about three minutes, until Zoe sidled up to him with the batter. The moment he caught her light floral scent with a hint of something muskier, he lost it.

He switched off the stove and turned to face her. Her eyes widened as she caught sight of the wildness that must have been reflected in his tortured gaze.

"I said pancakes first—"

"Fuck the pancakes."

At least he took the time to remove the batter bowl from her hands and place it on the counter before hoisting her onto it.

He spread her legs and buried his face between them. Licked her. Savored her low groan as he swiped his tongue over her clit and delved between her moist folds. He'd never tasted anything so sweet.

His cock pulsed with the need to be buried deep inside where his tongue currently probed. So he unzipped and freed himself. Stroked his cock while he licked her. Desperate to hold back the escalating tension.

"That is so fricking hot," she murmured, and as he glanced up, he saw her watching him.

In response, he lapped at her, increasing the pressure with his tongue, varying the speed, until she was panting and writhing.

"Dom, oh my God, yeah," she screamed, her fingers digging into his scalp as she came.

On the verge himself, he didn't waste any time. He sheathed himself in record time, then reached for her hips and tugged her to the edge of the counter before slamming into her.

No finesse. No softness. Hard and fast like the first time. He couldn't seem to control his reaction to her unashamed sexuality, couldn't seem to focus on anything but being inside her tight wetness.

"More," she demanded, urging him on by clutching at his shoulders and wrapping her legs around his waist.

So he delivered. Pumping into her until he was mindless, caught up in the throes of an orgasm so powerful, he almost blacked out.

She convulsed around him a moment later, her passion-fogged gaze locked on his.

Dominic wanted to speak. He wanted to say how she made him feel: like a hormonal teenager who couldn't keep it in his pants around her. That she deserved to be romanced. Or at least indulged in hours worth of foreplay.

But he was rendered speechless by the expression in her eyes. Gratitude. And something else. Something akin to the same crazy, out-of-control feeling ricocheting through him, a feeling he had no hope of labeling, because he didn't have a frigging clue what it was.

"You know what this means, don't you?" She smiled and it lit up the room.

"What?"

"You owe me a double serving of pancakes."

Chapter Nine

Zoe couldn't move.

She lay sprawled on the way-too-comfy sofa, her stomach full of pancakes and maple syrup. How many had she demolished? Three? Five? She'd lost count after the sixth. Because as long as she kept her mouth full, she had no reason to talk. And that's one activity she really didn't want to do with Dominic within hearing distance: talk.

After what they'd done, first up against the hallway wall and less than ten minutes later on the kitchen counter? No, talking was out of the question, because Zoe may just say exactly what she was thinking...*holy sexed-up prince!*

She hated to admit, but in most of her sexual encounters, she was the one in charge. She knew what she liked and didn't hesitate in telling the guy how to get her off.

With Dominic? No. Words. Necessary.

No instructions or gentle guiding with her hands either. The man had a way with his tongue and his cock that defied belief.

He wanted. He took.

She liked that, too. Liked it a little on the rough side. There was a time and place for finesse, and the last hour hadn't been it.

With the storm raging outside, it was almost like they'd faced a tumultuous storm of their own. If she'd been horny, looked like the randy prince had been doubly so.

She'd been a fool to think they could ignore their sexual attraction, dance around the flirting, without eventually hitting breaking point.

So now that they'd passed that point, where to from here?

Zoe had a presentation to give. To nail. But how did she look the guy in the eye when the last time she'd done that, he'd had his face between her legs?

Like any guy worthy of the gender, he'd bolted to his man cave after their encore performance in the kitchen. She'd cooked the pancakes herself and scoffed most of them. So there'd been no awkward post-sex conversation, no confronting what needed to be said: that they put this behind them and move on to more professional ground.

Yeah, right.

Her stomach grumbled, and she rubbed it. She really shouldn't have had that last pancake. Just like she really shouldn't have had sex with Dominic.

Man, Allegra would have a fit when she heard...Zoe reached for her cell before realizing the storm hadn't abated, so contact with the outside world would be via the satellite phone she'd spied in the hallway. And the last thing she felt like doing was articulating the mess she'd made of this business opportunity to her BFF.

Damn. She may have fucked royalty, but she was the one who'd ended up royally fucked.

"Thanks for cooking the pancakes; they were great." Dominic entered the lounge and chose the seat farthest away from her.

"Do I have girl cooties?" She pretended to sniff at her armpits, silently grateful he hadn't sat close. The last thing she needed right now was a repeat of the last time they'd gotten too cozy. Not that she wouldn't enjoy it. But she needed to establish boundaries, and getting naked with Dominic wouldn't achieve that.

"I think we both know what will happen if I sit next to you," he said, the instant flare of heat in his steady gaze garnering a response from her way down, and she struggled not to squirm.

"That's what we need to talk about." She sat up, clasped her hands in her lap, and tried to look semiprofessional. "It can't happen again."

Far from appearing disappointed, he relaxed into the chair. "Why not?"

"Because it was an aberration. A spontaneous, irresponsible act between two people annoyed with each other and venting their frustration physically..." She trailed off, hoping he'd buy her holier-than-thou speech.

By the smirk playing about his mouth, he didn't. "Yes, it was spontaneous. And yes, we seem to annoy each other. But an aberration?" He shook his head. "Don't demean what we shared."

Hell. She'd expected him to agree with her. To gloss over the stupendous sex and move on to business. His resistance? Not conducive to her plans to focus on work.

"What we shared meant nothing beyond lust." She dusted off her hands. "Now that itch is scratched, we can move on."

"You're asking me to forget it?" He leaned forward and braced his forearms on his knees. "Because that's impossible, *cara*." His hypnotic stare made her flush all over. "Sex with you surpassed my fantasies."

Yikes.

She swallowed. "You've been fantasizing about me?"

Wrong question, dumbass. It sounded nothing like "Are you ready to hear my pitch?" The question she should've asked.

He nodded. "Since the moment we met on the castle grounds." His bold gaze roved over her body, making her breasts tingle and the rest of her throb with longing. "I like how you say what you think. And you don't hide behind coyness. It's refreshing." Her nipples tightened to peaks as he stared at her breasts before tearing his gaze away. "And I would like to continue."

"Continue what?"

As if she needed to ask. She could see exactly what he wanted, and in any other situation the feeling would be entirely mutual. But she couldn't afford to muddy business with pleasure. Not with so much at stake.

"Having phenomenal sex with you." He gestured at the window. "I miscalculated. This storm won't pass today. It may not even pass tomorrow. In which case we'll be stuck indoors 'til it clears, and I can give you a tour of the island. So between now and then, I propose we indulge our mutual passion."

Zoe would like nothing better. But he'd forgotten the most important indoor activity they could do: signing off on her proposal, the biggest advertising coup for the agency since they'd landed Kai Kaluna.

She needed Dom to agree to her advertising campaign. It was the only way she could prove herself: to Allegra, to her coworkers, to the residual inner doubt demon that never let up with the "you majorly fucked up once; you'll do it again."

"What about my pitch?"

He drummed his fingers against his thighs, pretending to think. "We make a trade. I'll listen to your presentation tomorrow if you give me the rest of the evening in bed."

"You're *blackmailing* me into sleeping with you?"

Like she needed her arm twisted. She'd be naked and straddling him in two seconds flat given the opportunity.

"Let's call it gentle persuasion," he said, his grin triumphant. "This evening, I want to take my time with you, *cara*. I want to strip you, shower with you, and take hours to explore your body with my mouth and my hands."

His eyes darkened to midnight. "I want to pleasure you repeatedly. Want to tease you. Want to take you over and over 'til dawn."

Wow. Simply wow.

How could Zoe say no in the face of such sensual honesty? "You should've been a diplomat with that silver tongue," she said, trying not to show how much his words had affected her.

She wasn't used to guys being so overtly...*sexual*. The American guys she'd slept with rated dinner, movie, drinks, and five minutes of foreplay as their wooing repertoire. But having Dominic articulate exactly what he wanted to do to her was the best foreplay she'd ever had.

"My tongue is all yours for as long as we're here, if you want it."

Oh, she wanted. Despite all her self-talk of the last few minutes, despite all the logical, rational reasons she shouldn't have sex with him again. Man, did she want.

"So you'll hear my presentation in full tomorrow morning?"

"Make it the afternoon." He stood and held out his hand to her. "I think we'll both need to sleep in tomorrow."

Zoe rarely hesitated. She knew what she wanted out of life and wasn't afraid to go out and grab it. But as she stared at Dominic's hand, she knew accepting his proposition had danger written all over it.

A few wild, impulsive sexual encounters could be written off as satisfying urges. Spending an entire night in his arms had the power to undermine her completely.

She avoided intimacy. Intimacy led to dependency and emotional instability and heartache. She should know. She'd seen it firsthand, growing up with parents who gave any connection beyond superficial a bad name.

"*Cara?*"

"I'm not your darling," she muttered, finally standing and placing her hand in his.

"For tonight, you will be." He raised her hand to his lips, turned it over, and placed a soft kiss in her palm before curling her fingers over it.

Yeah, she was royally fucked.

Chapter Ten

As Dominic lit the final candle and surveyed the bedroom, he was surprised to find he was nervous.

He had aced his Oxford finals, had presented to European delegations at economic summits, and had mingled easily with fellow royalty. Nerves were as foreign to him as the woman taking a bath in the next room.

What was it about Zoe Keaton that made him feel so off-kilter?

She'd been right. They shouldn't do this again. Should've attributed their first few explosive encounters as lust between two people who didn't trust or necessarily like each other. Fuck, he'd labeled her a leech, and she'd called him on it.

But despite every innate defense mechanism warning him she was a user like everyone else, he couldn't deny her other qualities. Her honesty was reassuring. He liked how she didn't mince words. And he sure as hell liked how she demonstrated what she wanted.

No, this wasn't anything to do with her. It was him. Ever since she'd marched into his castle like she owned the place, he'd been a little off-balance. Nothing overt, but he felt it, with the kind of deep-down instincts that told him he shouldn't allow tourists to overrun this part of the world.

Not that he would tell Zoe that yet. Plenty of time to let her down gently after she'd done her presentation.

It would be tough. Damn tough, looking into those big brown eyes and dashing her dreams. But she must have a plethora of other options, other clients to advertise for, so it wouldn't make or break her one way or the other.

He'd done his research. While her firm AW Advertising had gone through a shaky patch not that long ago after losing several major clients, landing Kai Kaluna's worldwide resorts had been a coup that rocketed the agency straight to the top. Interestingly, it looked like Zoe had been made partner only recently, which explained her gung-ho attitude. Her presentation to him would be her first as a partner, and it stood to reason she'd want to secure the deal. But if the founder, Allegra Wilks, trusted Zoe enough to make her a partner, it wasn't likely she'd fire her if things didn't go so well.

And sadly for Zoe, his plans and hers were worlds apart. The door creaked open, and Dominic took a deep breath, surreptitiously swiping his palms down the side of his pants. He'd showered and changed, wanting to make amends. Wanting to show her he could be a tender, considerate lover, not the sex-crazed maniac who liked it rough-and-ready whenever he felt like it.

"Nice," she said, glancing around the room as she stepped inside and shut the door. "Aromatherapy candles to get me in the mood, huh?"

"Neither of us needs help in that department," he said, willing himself to stand still and not bolt across the room to haul her into his arms.

She looked amazing in an ivory satin nightgown that ended mid-thigh, its sheen highlighting her skin perfectly. She glimmered in the candlelight. Incandescent. He'd never seen anything so beautiful.

"You're staring." She squared her shoulders, enjoying the attention, and the flimsy spaghetti straps holding her nightgown together tugged, highlighting her breasts.

"I can't look away."

His simple truth made her lips curve into a coy smile. "Just so you know, all that posh romantic stuff you say? Goes to my head."

"No man has ever said such things to you?"

She laughed, but it sounded bitterer than amused. "Trust me, you're way ahead of the field in the romance stakes."

"But I thought...I mean, the way I was forceful... earlier...ah, *testa di cazzo*," he said, every inch a dickhead, stumbling over his words like an adolescent.

"I have no idea what you just said, but I love it when you speak Italian." She padded toward him and he held his breath. "As for earlier? When we went at like a couple of sex-starved lunatics? I liked it. A lot. So don't think I need all the romance stuff, because I don't. I like it, but I don't need it."

She stopped a foot away, her honesty blowing him away. "Then what do you need?"

He wanted her to say "you." He willed her to say "you."

"This." She placed a hand over his heart, and it bucked beneath her palm.

He knew she hadn't meant that she wanted his heart, that all she wanted was to touch him. But for an insane moment, he was actually disappointed she didn't want him for more.

"I'm all yours," he said, deliberately standing still, curious to see what she would do next.

He'd been in control during their first two encounters, and he wanted to see what she'd do. Would Zoe be as bold in the bedroom as she was verbally?

"You're a brave man, putting yourself in my hands," she said, sliding her palm downward until it rested above his hard cock. "Aren't you afraid I'll have my wicked way with you?"

"A guy can always live in hope," he said, and she laughed, a genuinely happy sound that made something in his chest twang.

He hadn't experienced many chest twangs in his lifetime. He'd mistakenly thought his heart belonged to Lilia at one stage, but he'd never been as hot for her as he was for Zoe. Not that that amounted to much. Just meant Zoe turned him on, and once he'd had a taste, he couldn't get enough. He had a serious case of lust. Stupid, comparing an island fling with Zoe to his relationship with Lilia. But the fact that he'd been engaged to Lilia and had never wanted her as badly as he wanted Zoe probably spoke volumes.

"You know I'm going to make you beg, right?" Her fingers toyed with the hem of his T-shirt before she peeled it upward and over his head. "I'm going to love having a prince bowing at my feet."

"You just want me kneeling, because that aligns my tongue with your—"

She kissed him, a soft brush of her lips against his. A kiss designed to tease. To titillate. To drive a guy insane with wanting her.

He tried to deepen the kiss, but she wouldn't let him, deliberately easing away, only to kiss him again before their lips broke contact completely. Her hands skimmed his chest, his back, and lingered on his waist, toying with his waistband.

Her feather-light touch was as soft as her kisses, and it was driving him wild. He gritted his teeth against the urge to pick her up, throw her on the bed, and enter her.

Fuck, where did these caveman tendencies come from whenever he was around her?

She trailed kisses toward his ear, where she whispered, "Ready to beg yet?"

"If it'll get you naked, absolutely."

"So much for romantic declarations," she said, nibbling on his earlobe.

A fierce need to possess her ripped through him, but he clenched his hands into fists to prevent himself from grabbing her. He could do this. Could let her call the shots. Could control his rampant libido that sat up and howled every time she got within two feet of him.

As she toyed with his zipper, he blurted, "I lied."

She stilled. "About?"

"About wanting to take it slow." He stepped away, putting some much-needed distance between them before he lost it completely. "At the risk of sounding like an absolute idiot, there's something about you that makes me go a little nuts."

"Nuts is good. Especially these." She reached out to cup him in response, and he yelped. "We're on the same page. That's a start."

"See, there you go again." He jabbed a finger in her direction. "With your quick-fire wit and sassiness and intelligence. Making me want you more than is good for me."

"News flash, Your Hot Highness." She waved a hand between them. "I'll never be good for you. So let's settle for me being bad, okay?" She stepped forward, bringing her within tantalizing touching distance again. "Trust me. Me being bad can only be good."

She placed two hands on his chest and shoved, hard. Hard enough that he toppled backward onto the bed. He laughed, and damn, it felt great. Zoe stood over him, a wicked grin playing about her mouth.

"Now watch." She plucked at the little knotted bows on her shoulders, and the spaghetti straps unraveled. The nightie slithered to the floor, leaving her gloriously, eye-poppingly naked.

He'd been a dumbass, taking her hard and fast earlier. Because without disrobing, he'd missed out on *this*.

Zoe had curves. Womanly curves. Generous C cups. Smaller waist. Wider hips. Then she did a deliberate twirl, and he almost leaped off the bed.

Her ass was perfection.

She slowly turned back to face him, one eyebrow raised. "How's that for bad?"

"More," he demanded, his lungs seizing as she placed her hand over his cock.

"You didn't say please." Her fingernails scraped over his zipper, rasping over the metal, deliberately grazing his cock but not freeing him.

"Please," he said through gritted teeth, propping himself on his elbows to watch as she snagged the zip tab and gave it a little tug.

"That sounded mighty close to begging, so I'll play nice." She snapped the top button open and eased the zipper down.

He craved her touch like a madman. After what seemed like an eternity later, she slipped her hand inside and touched him. A slow, deliberate stroke that started at his balls, slid up his shaft, and squeezed his head.

He groaned, a desperate sound that matched how he was feeling. Desperate for her.

"At the risk of your ego swelling as big as this"—she squeezed him again—"your crown jewels are seriously impressive."

"Glad you approve," he managed to say, as she eased his pants over his waist and shimmied them down his legs, before flinging them away.

"That's better." She stared at him, her hungry gaze gobbling him from head to foot, like she couldn't get enough. "Much better."

She looked away for a moment and spied the condoms he'd left on the bedside table.

"I want to pleasure you—"

"Later," she said, placing a fingertip to his lips. "I believe you promised me all night?" She leaned over and plucked a foil packet from the stack. "But for now, we do this my way."

"As you wish."

She smiled at his formal response. A smile that grew positively impish as she ripped the foil with her teeth, slid the condom out, and rolled it over him with exquisite, torturous precision.

"Watch out, Dom, things are about to get real bad," she said, climbing onto the bed to straddle him.

"I'm all for bad," he said, reaching for her breasts, but she swatted him away.

"Look, but don't touch." She cupped her breasts, as if offering them to him. "For now," she added, tweaking a nipple with one hand, the other sliding lower to rest over her Brazilian.

"I like it when you call me Dom," he said, unable to tear his gaze away from the sight of Zoe touching herself.

For that's exactly what she was doing while poised over him. Fingering herself. Touching her clit. Getting off. And damned if it wasn't the most exciting fucking thing he'd ever seen.

"Haven't had a nickname before?" She lowered herself a fraction, and her wet entrance brushed the head of his cock. "Because Dom suits you. Dominant. Domineering. Dominion."

"You can call me any damn thing you like, *cara*, but right now, I need to be inside you." He thrust upward a little, as her finger on her clit picked up the pace.

"Your wish is my command, Your Horny Highness," she said, sliding down inch by delicious inch, impaling herself on him.

"Horny Highness?" He laughed, probably for the first time during sex. It felt good. Natural. "Think I prefer Dom."

"Me, too." Her knees squeezed his hips as she lifted up, then slid down again, maintaining a slow, deliberate rhythm that sent him insane.

He craved taking it fast, pumping into her until the relentless tension spiraling through his body released.

But he lay there, obeying orders. Not touching her. Letting her set the pace. Watching her touch herself.

And wondering the entire time where this amazing woman had been all his life.

"I think I've been bad enough," she said, pumping her hips faster. "Now it's time for the good part."

As he watched, she continued to pleasure herself, managing to hold back her orgasm until the pressure in his balls built, and he exploded with a guttural groan. Only then did she push herself over the edge, her cries mingling with his as they slowly came back down to earth.

He finally gave in to the urge to reach for her. She hesitated a second before allowing him to pull her down to lie on top of him, her head nestled in the crook of his neck.

"*Cara?*"

"Hmm?"

"Give me five minutes, then I think it's my turn to be bad."

"Deal," she murmured, snuggling into him, and for the first time since he'd thrown reservations to the wind and had sex with Zoe, he wondered how something so wrong, so fleeting, so transiently fun, could feel so damn right.

Chapter Eleven

Zoe sat at the dining table, perusing her notes one last time before presenting to Dom.

Because that's how she'd always think of him after last night. Dom. Relaxed. Sensual. A sexual god. Dominic was far too formal. And nothing like the laid-back guy she'd had sex with five times last night.

He made her less nervous. But if he strutted into this room and had reverted to the surly arrogant prick he'd been when they'd met, she was in so much trouble.

Like she wasn't already.

The storm still raged outside, but it was nothing compared with the one she waged against herself. It was one thing to be seduced last night, but in the harsh reality of today, she knew connecting with Dom on an intimate level would only make her job harder.

She prided herself on thorough research, but nowhere in her search on the prince had she learned that his gruff exterior hid a tenderness with the potential to make her come undone.

Zoe didn't fall for the guys she had sex with. She didn't feel much of anything barring the pleasure her body craved. But last night with

Dom had far surpassed any previous sexual encounter and catapulted her straight into forbidden territory. A place where romance existed and hearts got broken. A place she'd never visit if she had her way.

Intimacy was for schmucks. She never should've allowed last night to happen. Because the fact that she was even thinking about Dom as more than a sex object this morning meant he'd moved from sexual conquest to interesting guy in her head.

Screw intimacy and romance and all the associated bullshit that went with it.

She'd seen it all before with her folks. The way her dad would shower her mom with gifts and attention, but only as a way to soothe his guilty conscience. Her mom would lap it up, then fall into a depression when her dad moved on to his next shiny toy or became work-obsessed again.

It was a cycle she'd seen repeatedly over the years, had hated growing up in what felt like a war zone at times: her mom hiding her tears but withdrawing emotionally from her only child, her dad showering her with gifts, too, to make up for his long absences from home.

To this day, Zoe didn't know if her dad had been unfaithful to her mom. But the fact that he found drilling for oil more stimulating than his wife ensured Zoe grew up with a moody mom and a dad who didn't have a clue how to be a good husband and father.

She didn't know what was worse: watching her mom primp and pander when her dad did show up, desperate for whatever scraps of affection he'd throw her way, or the resultant fallout when he eventually left again and her mom reverted to a sniveling shell of her former self with no pride.

No great surprise Zoe had vowed from a young age never to be that weak. She would never fall so hard for a guy she became emotionally dependent on him for happiness. She would make her own rules. She would be the one in control. And it had suited her just fine.

Until last night.

Because despite her dominant act the first time they'd had sex in the bed, Zoe knew deep down she wasn't in control. Not any more.

In making her feel so good, Dom had usurped her power. He knew how she liked to be licked, touched, caressed. He knew the scar on her right butt cheek had been the result of an embarrassing rollerblading incident when she'd landed on a wire fence at age fourteen. He knew her most erogenous zones were the ticklish spots behind her knees. He knew she liked it hard and fast and a little wild. Because that way, she could lose herself in the physical act and not be swayed by sweetness and tenderness.

That had been her mistake last night, allowing Dom to make love to her. Not the rough-and-ready sex she preferred, but a slow, sensual experience that had started with a leisurely exploration of her body and ended with the best head of her life. Three times. Before he slid into her. And he'd kept at it all night. Battering her defenses. Seducing her with whispered words and tender caresses. She hadn't stood a chance.

The damnedest thing was, how could something that was a mistake feel so good and make her feel like she was floating on air today?

She scrolled through the final pages of her presentation, confident she could recite the thing in her sleep. Which might not be such a bad idea if Dom didn't go for her pitch today. She might have better luck coercing him in the bedroom tonight. Because according to the weather forecast he'd picked up via satellite phone this morning, they'd be stuck here for at least another day or two. Looked like even Catarina had underestimated the power of this storm. "One in a century" they were labeling it, which made Zoe increasingly grateful they'd reached the safety of this cottage before the thing had hit.

So another two days cooped up with Dom...last night may have been a mistake, allowing him to sneak under her defenses, but Zoe wasn't a complete fool. She knew there'd be a repeat tonight and tomorrow. No point playing coy now. But she better steel herself against his charm, because the way Dom could make a woman feel in the bedroom? Something she could seriously get used to. And that would be a pointless exercise in self-flagellation. She wasn't her mom, easily swayed by compliments and a little affection.

"Ready?" Dom strode into the room, and every cell in Zoe's body snapped to attention. She could practically feel her synapses zinging in remembrance.

"Uh-huh," she managed to say, gathering her documents into a neat pile and ensuring her presentation had the first slide ready to go.

She hadn't looked at him yet, would delay the moment for as long as possible. Because how did she look a guy she'd had sex with seven times in less than twenty-four hours in the eye and pretend like this was all business?

"Let's get started then." He took a seat opposite her, and she finally glanced up, unprepared for the surge of longing as their gazes locked, coupled with a desire to crawl across the table and sit in his lap.

He appeared calm and in control and incredibly handsome in a white button-down shirt open at the collar, its crispness highlighting his tan and the bright blue of his eyes. Zoe wanted to say something funny, something lighthearted to break the invisible tension sizzling between them. But she couldn't look away long enough to get her brain to work in sync with her mouth.

"You have to stop looking at me like that," he said, his lips curving into a devastating smile.

"Like what?"

Hell, was she that easy to read?

"Like you want to devour me for breakfast," he said, nudging a fruit bowl toward her. "Here. Have a banana instead."

By the wicked spark in his fiery gaze, he was deliberately baiting her. Trying to throw her off her game. Well, two could play at that.

"Maybe I will."

She selected the largest, longest banana. Unpeeled it. Then slowly eased it into her mouth, wrapping her lips around it like it was the most delicious thing she'd ever tasted.

"Mmm..." She didn't take a bite. Instead, she withdrew the banana slightly and rolled her tongue over the tip.

"You're playing with fire," he said, his tone low and husky.

"Actually, I'm just having a snack before we get started," she said, resisting the urge to laugh as his eyes flared at her innuendo.

"Just hurry up and eat the damn thing." He tore his tortured gaze away to stare out the window.

She knew the feeling. She'd give anything to say screw the presentation and screw him instead. But she had to do this. Her future depended on it.

She demolished the banana, grateful for the sugar hit. "Okay, I'm ready."

He looked back while surreptitiously readjusting himself beneath the table, and she couldn't resist teasing him one last time. "For what it's worth? That banana was a poor substitute."

He half rose, and she waved him back down. "You promised you'd listen to my pitch this morning."

He hesitated, the heat in his eyes scorching her clear across the table, before he sank back down again. "Fine. But that little performance you just gave? Deserves payback. Later."

She gulped. Later couldn't come quick enough.

"From your grandmother's e-mails to me, you've had contact with Kaluna's developer, so you know what Kaluna wants to do with the expansion of his resort." She slid several documents across the table. "So all I've done here is reiterate the main points of the ecological studies he's undertaken, highlighting minimal change to the surrounding area, which I'll expand on further in the ad pitch."

Dom barely glanced at the documentation, and her heart sank. She needed him to take her seriously, needed him on board for this to work. Maybe hard figures would impress him more.

"And if you turn to page three of the financial report, you'll see estimates of the income the projected boost in tourism would bring to the area."

She waited until he looked at the relevant page, a zap of relief piercing her nervousness when she saw his eyebrows rise at the figures quoted. "That's a sizable amount of money."

She nodded. "And it doesn't stop there. Visitors to Ancora can only come here via Osturo, so this worldwide ad campaign will ultimately fill Osturo's coffers too."

"Indeed," he said, his tone void of any emotion.

She tried not to let his apathy get to her. "With the campaign, we're willing to work with your advisers one-on-one, ensuring we highlight the areas of the islands you want."

She swiped her finger across the tablet several times to bring up the relevant slide: the last slide he'd seen before he'd walked out on her yesterday morning.

Crap, had it only been a day earlier that they'd been at loggerheads? So much had happened in twenty-four hours, and not all of it good. This uncharacteristic floundering feeling? So foreign as to be alien. She needed to get a grip. Fast. And get Dom to sign on the dotted line.

"My firm will ensure a tailor-made campaign that benefits Kaluna and you." She flicked through a few mock-ups. "These are just to give you a general feel of what AW Advertising can do, but like I said, we'll work closely with you."

She'd spent an inordinate amount of time on the mock-ups. Had focused on the eco-angle that all Kaluna's resorts were famous for. She'd used pictures of Ancora gleaned off the Internet and made the island look like a paradise no sane person could resist. She wanted to show him what could be if he opened himself up to the possibilities. Wanted to tempt him to align himself with Kaluna and benefit them all.

"Impressive," he said, barely glancing at the prelims she'd worked hours on, making it sound like it was anything but.

Damn, he was a hard sell.

"This ad campaign will keep these islands profitable for years—"

"What if I say no?"

Annoyed by his rude interruption, she glared at him. "We're hoping you're not that shortsighted."

"Insults are beneath you," he said, reverting to the cold, arrogant bastard he'd been when they'd met, and Zoe knew she was on the verge of blowing her cool, blowing this presentation, and blowing her future.

She never should have blown him.

"I can see the work you've put into this." He gestured at her tablet and documentation. "You've done a great job."

"But?"

There was a huge "but" coming. She could hear it in his somber tone, see it in his rigid, defensive posture.

"But I'm not going to be swayed into making any hasty decisions." He steepled his fingers and rested his elbows on the table. "I'm in charge of what happens with these islands, and I take my responsibility seriously."

"Never said you didn't," she muttered, wondering how an Oxford-educated, well-traveled, economically astute, twenty-first-century monarch could sound so archaic.

She'd hoped to wow him with her presentation, have a tour of Kaluna's resort, and get him to agree to their terms in less than seven days. By his mutinous expression, she'd been deluding herself.

So he was a hard sell? She could handle him. How many times had she done the background work for Allegra with clients just as recalcitrant as Dom? Allegra always said having the incredible inside knowledge Zoe's research provided helped land those tough-sell clients, so it had to work this time. It had to.

That persistent niggling doubt, about the recent deal where she'd done a huge amount of background research on their oldest clients but lost them anyway? Something she couldn't afford to acknowledge now. Not when she was on the verge of losing this mega-campaign before it had begun.

Maybe she needed to delve deeper into Dom's background to discover the crucial information she needed to sway him? With no

Internet access, online research was impossible. But she had the man himself at her disposal. How would he react with a little subtle probing? Probably not well, but only one way to find out.

"You're against Kaluna expanding his resort and an advertising campaign that will flood this island with tourists." She shut down her presentation, shuffled her documents together, and pushed them aside in an attempt to get him to speak off the record. "Is there a specific reason?"

His lips flattened into an unimpressed line. So much for getting him to talk.

"I can understand your environmental concerns, which are noble, by the way." Hopefully flattery would get her everywhere. "But you've seen how well Kaluna has blended his resort with the natural habitat on Ancora already. He's good at what he does. He's won awards for it from major tourism organizations around the world. So why the reservations—"

"Ancora has always been my family's getaway," he said, glancing away to stare at some point over her shoulder. "It was a private island. Unspoiled. A place to escape to."

Ah...now Zoe was getting somewhere. Was Ancora his go-to place? Growing up, her place to shun reality had been the local library. When her dad was away on a drilling site and her mom's moroseness got to be too much, she'd spend hours at the library, lost in the pages of a paranormal young-adult novel.

Kids used to laugh at her, the bookworm rebel. She'd do tequila shots and smoke at parties on the weekend but could be found in the library night after night. Those books had comforted her better than chocolate, and even now, she couldn't walk past a library without wanting to spend an afternoon in a carrel.

Years later, when she'd moved to LA, the musty smell of a used book instantly made her feel safe. Is that how Dom felt here?

She wanted to ask, but knew he'd clam up if she went for his jugular straight-up, so she skirted around the issue.

"Do you resent your grandfather allowing Kaluna to build a resort here? Is that it?"

He shook his head, pain clouding his eyes, and her heart clenched at the underhanded way she was going about getting info, any info, that could prove useful in her securing this campaign.

"Nonno trusted Kaluna. They had a gentleman's agreement." His gaze shifted back on to her, and she struggled not to squirm under that all-too-astute stare. "He had a good instinct for people. Summed them up on first meeting just like that." He snapped his fingers. "I'm the same."

Uh-oh. Considering how brazen she'd been when they'd met on the castle grounds, what did Dom really think of her?

His mouth relaxed into a semblance of a smile. "You're wondering what I thought of you when we first met."

Her initial instinct was to lie, but that wouldn't help her cause of getting him to trust her enough to divulge more. "Maybe a little?" She held up her thumb and forefinger an inch apart.

"You're intelligent. And articulate. And bold. I like that." The steely glint in his eyes faded. "Honesty is a trait I value highly. It's all-important to me. So I liked how blunt you've been in our...dealings to date."

He was talking about their sex antics. She could see it in the relaxing of his posture, the softening around his mouth. But she couldn't afford to get off track, and that's exactly what responding with a flirtatious comment right now would achieve.

"So keeping with your honesty theme, why don't you want to continue what your grandfather started?" She pointed out the window. "Not that I've seen much of the island yet thanks to that brutal storm out there, but if he had the foresight to deal with Kaluna in the first place, shouldn't you do the same?"

He stiffened, the partial smile vanishing. "Because I'm not my grandfather."

"You're trying to assert your dominance?" She was treading on dangerous ground, but she'd started down this path; she had to continue. "Is that what this is about? You're deliberately wanting to do the opposite of him?"

His eyes narrowed to fiery blue slits. "You don't know anything about me."

"Maybe I'd like to." She threw it out there casually, alluding to more than their business dealings.

Because if Zoe were completely honest with herself, she did want to know more about this enigmatic man. No guy she'd ever dated, even the ones she'd been involved with for longer than a few weeks, had intrigued her as much as Dom. Which is exactly why she should focus on business.

"Let's not pretend this is something that it's not." He waved a hand between the two of them. "You and I share a powerful sexual connection. One I would like to keep exploring while we're stuck in each other's company—"

"Wow, when you put it like that, how could any woman refuse?"

He ignored her droll response and continued. "But we both know there is no future for us, so please don't try to patronize me by suggesting otherwise."

For an insane moment, Zoe felt like crying. So she fell back on her surefire way to deflect emotions. "You obviously don't have too many friends, because you'd know that's what people do when they're getting to know each other, for a week or otherwise. They chat. They talk about personal stuff. That's all I meant by saying I'd like to know more, okay?"

On a roll, she puffed up with indignation, the words pouring out of her mouth. "But thanks for the clarification. You want to fuck me, but you don't want to know anything else. Got it."

She held up her hand and pretended to write on it with the other. "No niceties. No politeness. No mistaking a connection in the bedroom for anything other than a cheap fu—"

"That's enough." He stood so fast the chair toppled. "Don't belittle what we have."

"Why not? You just did." She leaped to her feet too, wishing she could lean across the table and stab him in the chest with a fingernail. "I guess we're done here."

Emotion clogged her throat, and she busied herself tidying her stuff before she burst into tears. She needed him to leave her alone, to give her some time to figure out where they went from here. Because her kick-ass presentation just went to hell in a hand-basket.

This was exactly what she didn't want. To *feel* anything for Dom. And that's what had happened when they'd connected on an intimate level last night. Sex she could handle. Making love? A stupendously bad idea.

How had she fucked up so badly?

She'd spent years holding men at bay emotionally, deliberately maintaining a fun, flirty facade to protect herself from feeling exactly how shitty she was right now.

"I'm sorry." He'd sneaked up behind her and laid a hand on her shoulder. "You didn't deserve any of that. I'm just not used to opening up to anyone."

She didn't want to turn, but he left her no option when he gently spun her around.

"I haven't been close to a woman since Lilia." The heartache in his tone finally made her glance up and meet his gaze. "I'm out of practice."

His sincerity undermined her almost as much as the sadness in his voice.

"So you're not some renowned playboy prince who masquerades as a recluse?" The quiver in her voice undercut her deliberately flippant remark.

Damn, she needed to get a grip before she cried and embarrassed the hell out of both of them.

"Don't believe everything you read about me online."

"You're not a recluse?"

He glanced away. "Socializing loses its appeal after a while."

"Yeah, I guess all those A-list parties and royalty-exclusive soirees and launching ships gets tiring."

Finally, the glimmer of a smile. "Princesses or queens usually launch ships."

"Too bad. I bet you'd be real good at smashing champagne bottles against bows."

"That's better." He reached up and trailed a fingertip across her bottom lip. "I like it when you're teasing and lighthearted."

"And I like it when you're open and receptive, not repressed and grumpy."

"There you go again, hitting me with your refreshing honesty right here." He grabbed her hand and pressed it over his heart in a gesture that made hers race like a wild thing. "And I can honestly say I've never wanted a woman more."

If Zoe's heart had been racing a moment ago, it fairly stopped at his mind-blowing declaration. She needed clarification before she read way more into that statement than was good for her.

"But what about Lilia? You were engaged to her?"

She watched the battle he waged within himself. Every conflicting emotion radiated from his eyes. Regret. Sadness. Wariness. Anger. She expected him to clam up, hoped he wouldn't.

"Lilia helped me through a hard time in my life." He tugged on her hand, and they both sat. She was impressed when he didn't release her. "The death of my parents hit me hard, and I was floundering. She made me laugh again. I was indebted to her."

For once, Zoe clamped down on her urge to blurt her first thoughts. The last thing Dom needed to hear was how making life-changing decisions while grieving probably wasn't ideal.

"I guess I became dependent on her for my happiness."

If anyone understood how that worked, it was Zoe. Her mom was the same with her dad, and it had turned her from a bubbly, bright woman to a sad, maudlin mess.

He rubbed the back of his neck. It did little to ease the obvious tension making his muscles stand to rigid attention. "But we were doomed from the start. We were too different. I loved the quiet island life; she loved the big cities. We started to drift apart before…"

Pain, raw and undiluted, contorted his features. "She died in a car crash. Sitting alongside the developer who'd been hounding me to sell off tracts of land I own."

The implication behind Dom's revelation detonated, and Zoe gripped his hand tight. "She was cheating on you?"

"I don't know." He shrugged. "But what she was doing was just as bad."

Confused, Zoe shook her head. "Like what?"

"Elio wanted to build condos on these islands and turn Osturo and Ancora into the next Ibiza." The sadness in his eyes solidified into fury. "She was feeding him information. Soil reports. Zoning permits. Copies of the land deeds. Everything."

"Oh my God..." Zoe couldn't believe any woman would be stupid enough to do something so treacherous, especially to her fiancé.

How Dom must've felt...the betrayal, the anger, mingling with sorrow at losing another person close to him.

"I'm sorry you had to go through something so painful." She leaned over and hugged him tight. "For what it's worth, she was a fool for choosing to hurt you in such a way."

"Thanks." He eased her away, held her at arm's length. "Now can you understand why I'm not so good with the 'getting to know you better' thing?"

"You're scared..." It clicked in that moment: why he was reclusive, why he held himself aloof, why he freaked out when she said she wanted to get to know him better.

A woman he loved had betrayed him when he was at his most vulnerable. No wonder he didn't want to open up to her, a virtual stranger. Whom he probably considered as yet another outsider who wanted something from him.

"Fear isn't very manly," he said, grazing her cheek with the back of his knuckles. "Let's settle for saying I have a healthy disregard for emotional attachment."

"That makes two of us."

Before he could ask her why, she rushed on. "The rest of my

presentation centers on a tour of the current Kaluna resort and demonstrating what the campaign will highlight." She nodded at her work materials. "Let's leave this for today, and hopefully we'll be able to get outside later today or tomorrow?"

"More likely tomorrow." He glanced out the window and frowned. "By the weather reports via the sat phone, this isn't abating for another twenty-four hours."

"Wow, your grandmother really miscalculated—" Damn, the moment the words spilled from her lips, Zoe wished she could take them back.

"What does Nonna have to do with the weather?"

Considering what he'd just told her, about his fiancée's betrayal, Zoe knew this would look bad. With the help of his grandmother, she'd manipulated the situation for her gain. Getting Dom to sign on the dotted line would be a financial coup for her company and a huge win for her.

She crossed her fingers behind her back and hoped to God he wouldn't view her involvement in this crazy plot as a similar betrayal to Lilia.

"Uh…" Zoe couldn't lie, not after he'd praised her for being so honest. "Well, the whole kidnapping thing? It was kinda Catarina's idea."

Disappointment clouded his eyes. "An idea you were more than happy to go along with to further your agenda."

Yep, he was pissed at her. "I thought it was a pretty ingenious way to ensure your undivided attention."

"And underhanded," he added, not sounding amused in the least, before a reluctant smile erased his disenchanted expression. "Though it's typical Nonna at her crafty best."

He stared at her with disillusionment, and it didn't take an Einstein to figure out he'd bitten back the rest: "but what's your excuse?"

Increasingly uncomfortable that Dom now viewed her as being like his scheming ex, she said, "She knew the storm would be a doozy and we'd be stranded here for a day, so she thought that would make you my captive audience." Zoe waved at the storm still raging outside. "Guess she underestimated how bad it would be."

"Or did she?" Dom's eyes narrowed to slits of blue brilliance. "Nonna has lived on these islands all her life. She can predict the storms by the aches in her joints." He pointed at the window. "She would've known exactly how bad this storm would be."

"Then why strand us together for so long...? Ah, so my instincts were right." Zoe smiled. That devious old queen.

Dom nodded. "Nonna is a renowned matchmaker on the island. She thinks we'd be suited."

"You and me?" Zoe laughed, trying to alleviate Dom's bad mood since he'd learned the truth about being stranded. "As you said, there's no future for us. Why would she go to such lengths?"

His expression grew grimmer. "She's an old woman, and she's worried about me."

He stood, turned his back on her, and crossed to the window. "She'll hear my thoughts on her scheme when we return."

"Whereas I cop your bad mood now?" The words slipped out before she could stop them. Just what she needed, to antagonize him further.

His shoulders stiffened. "What did you expect? That I'd be thrilled you manipulated this situation to suit yourself?" He shook his head, and she only just heard, "Knew it was too good to be true."

Saddened that he'd lumped her in with the rest of the suck-ups who probably wanted something from him—even if she kinda deserved it—she said, "If it's okay with you, I'm going to spend the afternoon in my room." She gathered up her stuff, clutching it to her chest. "I'll skip lunch."

"Fine." By his icy tone, it wasn't.

"I'll see you later."

His chilly silence haunted her long after she'd reached the sanctity of her room.

Chapter Twelve

Dominic took refuge in the family room at the back of the house. He'd spent many hours here as a kid. Building model airplanes. Constructing elaborate forts and castles from blankets and chairs. And at night, playing cards and board games with his parents. They'd been a close family, and he hadn't minded being an only child. He'd lapped up the attention. And he admired them for raising him as a normal kid without the crown and title hanging over his head. He'd had to scoop up the family dog poop and weed the garden and tend to Nonna's veggie patch like any other kid. His parents had wanted it that way.

It wasn't until much later, when he'd attended Oxford, that he'd been grateful for the normality of his childhood. He'd mixed with students from many different walks of life there, and the majority of the upper-class ones had been utter pricks. Snobby, condescending bastards who'd looked down their noses at everyone, including the lecturers. Many of them had tried to get him on their side by schmoozing, but he'd made it clear from the start he didn't care about class distinctions. So they settled for ignoring him instead. Suited him just fine. The problem arose when the kids from less privileged backgrounds had tried sucking up to him, faking false friendship for anything from free holidays on his island to cash.

Their relentless, shameless pandering had made him plain uncomfortable. So he'd distanced himself. Become increasingly aloof. Withdrawing from everyone, until the users ended up ignoring him, too.

He'd pretended that he hadn't cared. Had studied hard and gotten exceptional grades. Had believed his self-talk that he preferred being a loner. But those nights when he heard the guys gathering outside the dorm to head into town for an evening of carousing at the pub, or when he wasn't invited to be part of a study group before exams, the loneliness crept up on him. And it had been palpable.

When he'd finished his degree and headed to London to make his mark as a businessman, he had socialized. Been open to invitations. But the protective mechanisms he'd honed to a fine art while at Oxford persisted, and he never allowed anyone too close. He suspected the motives of everyone who approached on the pretense of friendship, and he'd ended up more alone than ever. And all the while he'd wished he was back here, on Ancora, in this house, the only place he'd never had to keep up appearances.

He sank into his favorite chair, a faded blue chintz, and propped his ankles on the coffee table. The chair faced the window encapsulating the view he'd looked at for hours as a kid.

The rocky outcrops of Ancora's towering cliffs and the ocean beyond were still obscured by the lashing rain and dark, low-slung clouds, but he didn't mind. Just being here made him feel more grounded. Something he desperately needed after his run-in with Zoe that morning.

Eight hours later, he was still rattled.

Where had that ridiculous urge to unburden his soul come from? One minute she'd been delivering a sound proposal; the next he was blabbing about his failed engagement and his grandfather.

Shit.

Then to top it off, he'd discovered she'd manipulated this entire stranded scenario to further her cause. And she'd echoed what he knew was the truth: there was no future for them. He should've been happy she felt the same way he did. Ecstatic, in fact. Instead, a coldness had seeped through him that he hadn't been able to shake since.

And what had he done? Let her hide out in her room all afternoon, while he'd alternated between trying to read the latest bestselling spy thriller, mulling her presentation, and pacing the house. She hadn't come out of her room either, even when he'd knocked on the door and asked if she wanted dinner. She'd yelled out something about grabbing a bite of supper later but hadn't opened the door.

He'd been affronted. They'd been intimate, had really connected last night, and he'd thought…what? That a woman like Zoe would be happy having him open his big mouth and dump a load of blunt home truths, then tolerate his foul mood when he'd discovered her part in being stranded, yet expect her to jump into bed with him again tonight?

Deep down, that's exactly what he'd hoped. Only an arrogant bastard like him would treat a woman appallingly and still expect sex.

This was why he didn't do relationships. He was too shut off from people in general, let alone a vibrant, warm, beautiful woman who'd claimed to want the same thing he wanted to give. A few days of raunchy sex. Sounded great in theory. Shame his practice sucked.

If he had any balls, he'd whip up some of those pancakes she loved and knock on her bedroom door. Try to pick up where they'd left off, physically. But considering the mood he'd been in when they left things this morning, she'd brand his balls with the pointy end of her pumps.

No, best to leave Zoe alone and consider ways to make it up to her tomorrow. The weather should clear by the late morning, and he intended on giving her the grand tour of the island. After that, maybe a picnic?

WANTON HEAT

He knew just the spot. The lagoon. Secluded. Stunning.

Perfect for seduction if he was so inclined.

And he was. He grew hard visualizing Zoe swimming naked with him...

His balls? Would be blue by tomorrow.

Chapter Thirteen

"This place is unbelievable," Zoe said, holding her arms wide and spinning on the spot. "Who would've thought that shocking weather the last few days could conceal something like this?"

Dominic stared at her, unable to tear his eyes away. She practically glowed, her sun-kissed face tilted to the sun, her eyes bright and appreciative, her smile as wide as the ocean surrounding them.

They'd been hiking for thirty minutes in silence following the awkwardness of yesterday, taking a little-known path through the bush to reach Kaluna's resort. He'd deliberately brought her this way rather than sailing the boat around to the main jetty near the hotel, because he wanted to show her his favorite spots. Wanted to gauge her reaction, truth be known.

And she hadn't disappointed. Thankfully, the beauty of his favorite island had gotten them past their mutual unease.

She'd ooh'd and aah'd over the scenery, the foliage, and now the lookout. Almost the highest point on the island, the 360-degree view was nothing short of spectacular. As was Zoe.

To see her laughing, joyful, so full of life, made his chest ache. He wanted to be that carefree. That impulsive. That alive. And the longer he stared at her, the more that terrifying ache in his chest expanded. It shouldn't. He didn't want it to. But there was something about her vibrancy that was infectious.

Simply, he liked the way she made him feel.

Even after the sleepless night he'd had, when he'd tossed and turned, debating whether to sneak into her room like a horny teenager, her excitement at seeing Ancora for the first time was contagious.

He loved this place and to have her share that with him...well, damned if he didn't want to sweep her into his arms and never let go.

Foolish, errant thought. It had no place in his logical head. But it was there all the same, as taunting as Zoe wearing denim cutoff shorts that accentuated her pert ass and a turquoise tank top that molded to her like a second skin.

They had to make it to Kaluna's resort damn quick, before he ravished her here and now.

"I'm glad you like it." Great. King of the understatement.

"I love it." She did another twirl before staring at him with eyes so wide he could see the sun picking out the caramel flecks in the brown depths. "Remind me to thank your grandmother for making me kidnap you and ending up stranded here."

He could've bristled again at the reminder of Zoe's part in the harebrained scheme. Instead, he took a deep breath and released any residual animosity. They had a short-term connection, nothing more. It may rankle that she wanted to benefit financially from their time together, but he'd be better off focusing on the perks—like their explosive chemistry.

"Technically? We're not stranded anymore." He pointed to the calm ocean and the private jetty where his boat was moored many miles below and to the east. "We can leave any time you're ready."

"Oh, no, you don't." She waggled her finger at him, and he clamped down the urge to kiss the tip, then slide the whole thing into his mouth. "You owe me a tour of the resort and then we talk business again. And I'm not leaving this island 'til you listen."

"What are you going to do? Tie me up?"

Something he imagined doing to her. He imagined her arms and legs splayed, tied to the old iron bedposts in the master bedroom. Her nipples would be hard, begging for his mouth. And she'd be wet, glistening, ready for him...

Fuck, not helping the situation.

"You wish." She winked and turned her back on him, continuing on the path that now led down toward the resort.

"You have no idea how much," he murmured, for his ears only.

And as Zoe maintained a steady chatter for the next fifteen minutes, exclaiming over the olive and lemon groves, the grapevines, and the birds, he listened in bemused silence. Contributing when he had to but content to let her excitement infuse him with passion. Not sexual passion. He had enough of that for her. More a passion for his island, for life.

He'd always loved this place but seeing it through her eyes made him appreciate it all the more. The best part? She wasn't faking it or trying the hard sell. She genuinely liked Ancora, and it made him contemplate scenarios he shouldn't.

Once their business concluded, maybe he should kidnap her for the next month or two.

Yeah, like that was going to happen. Reality check: Zoe would bolt as soon as he gave her his answer. A definitive no.

He couldn't tell her the truth about why he didn't want to go with her proposal, so she'd assume he was a stubborn, arrogant prick, and she'd leave ASAP. It was inevitable. It had happened countless times before, when those who wanted something from the Ricci family didn't get their way. They bolted. But it didn't make accepting it any easier.

Because sometime over the last few days, between her early arrival at the castle when she'd boldly ogled him, and kidnapping him on the boat, the feisty American had crept under his guard and wormed her way into his well-protected heart.

After all these years, he should be wiser. Damned if he didn't want to feel anything for her beyond a healthy sexual attraction. Sadly, what he wanted and what had happened were as far apart as their respective home countries.

Zoe was an LA girl; he was an Italian prince. A man with a vision that didn't match hers.

What they shared was nothing more than a potent, transient fling. It's what he had clearly articulated yesterday.

So why did he feel so goddamned shitty about it?

His cell buzzed in his back pocket, and he grabbed it, half hoping, half fearful it was the report from the PI he was waiting for. Hoping he'd get some info on Kaluna and Zoe, enough concrete evidence to send her packing. Fearful that he'd have to do just that.

Merda. This vacillating was shit. He was usually a decisive man, with no room for futile emotions. So why did his thumb shake as he swiped it across the phone screen to check his e-mails?

He released the breath he'd inadvertently been holding when he saw that the reminder e-mail was for a state dignitaries dinner in London next month and not the PI's report.

Yeah, this was definitely *merda*. He needed to get a grip on his uncharacteristic feelings before he really fucked up.

"We're here." She stopped at a white picket gate with a sign Private Property. Kaluna Resorts hanging off it. "Ready to be wowed by the rest of my pitch?"

"Everything you do wows me," he said, reverting to a little light-hearted flirtation to ease the tension gripping him.

Now that they were here, and Zoe could complete the final part of her presentation, he was feeling increasingly edgy. He would do the right thing and hear her out, couch his refusal in polite terms, and they'd part. It was inevitable from the beginning. Logical. So why did the thought of an untenable future make him feel this bad?

Her eyes narrowed. "You think flattery will put me off my game?"

He laughed, loving her ability to make him relax with a simple sentence. "You don't have a very high opinion of me, do you?"

"Let's just say you confuse the hell out of me," she said, softening the truth with a smile. "I can honestly say I've never met anyone like you, Dom Ricci."

That sounded good. Dom Ricci. No title. No formality. No responsibility. A guy could get used to that. Sadly, not him.

"Come on, I'll show you around." He unlatched the gate and held it open for her.

When she stepped through, she deliberately brushed her breasts against his chest, and he instantly hardened.

"What are you doing?"

"Giving you a little taste of what you'll be missing out on later today if you don't give me a fair hearing here." Her impish smile lit up her face.

"Now who's blackmailing who for sex?"

"Not blackmail. Consider it a little healthy incentive." With that, she wiggled her fingers in a jaunty wave over her shoulder and bounced ahead along the path.

That tightness in his chest? Spread until he could barely breathe, as for the first moment since he'd met Zoe, he wondered if there was the slightest chance in hell they could mesh their two visions for Ancora's future.

He couldn't trust her with the truth yet; he wasn't that foolish. But there would be definite advantages to working with Zoe.

The main one being keeping her in his life longer.

...

Zoe could see why Kai Kaluna wanted to spruce this place up.

While the resort resembled the layout of his signature Palm Bay

WANTON HEAT

resort in the South Pacific, where she'd scored the lucrative advertising contract alongside Allegra, it was showing its age. Faded terracotta exteriors courtesy of a scorching Mediterranean summer sun and the frequent storms like the doozy she'd been privy to. The kidney-shaped pool in need of retiling. Gardens that could do with a landscaping update. Fraying sun lounges and beach umbrellas that needed replacing. Staff uniforms that could be brought into the twenty-first century.

Nothing overt, but enough that her practiced eye picked up on the resort's faults. Her research gleaned that Dom's granddad had done a deal with Kaluna thirty years ago to build this resort, with the proviso that it was eco-friendly and didn't disturb the local environment. Kaluna had stuck to his end of the bargain, but the resort had blended so well with the island it had become almost invisible. And Dom's dad hadn't changed a thing since the old man had died twenty-five years ago. Profit margins were at an all-time low, and to capitalize on her glam million-dollar ad campaign, Kaluna had to expand.

That's where Dom came in.

He'd been surprisingly relaxed today. A welcome change after yesterday when she'd done her best to avoid him all afternoon and into the evening. She hadn't wanted to see him after their cozy chat following her presentation. Because if she had, she may have ended up reevaluating every sane reason why intimacy with a guy was so wrong for her.

Never had she imagined he'd disclose as much as he did. Worse, the effect it would have on her.

She'd wanted to hug him tight and never let go.

And if there was one thing Zoe never did, it was forever.

Amazing, how paparazzi and the world were so quick to label him surly and aloof when there was a very good reason for his withdrawal from society. He'd been grieving his parents' death when the person closest to him had ripped his heart out.

He'd been vulnerable, and that slut of a fiancée had betrayed him in the worst possible way. Zoe would lay odds the woman had been screwing his competitor, too. Otherwise, why would she be traveling in the guy's sports car along the Amalfi Coast? Checking out the scenery? Doubtful.

Zoe would give anything to bitch-slap the woman into oblivion for hurting Dom like that. He didn't deserve it. No one did. And it looked like the aftereffects of having his heart broken were lingering.

The guy didn't trust easily. She got that. What she didn't get was why he'd be so closed off in the business arena, too? Protecting his heart from female predators, she could understand. But why was he so mistrustful of change that could only help this island prosper?

His recalcitrance certainly stalled her plans. But now that they were here, and she'd had the grand tour, she had every intention of making him see sense.

"You're mentally preparing to give me another spiel, aren't you?" He sat beside her on a wrought iron bench overlooking the resort's stunning private beach.

"How can you tell?"

"You get this look." He made a face like a constipated bulldog. "Determination with a healthy dose of 'never say die.'"

She cocked her thumb and forefinger and mock-fired. "And don't you forget it."

"You're pretty hard to forget."

To her surprise, he bumped her with his shoulder, a strangely informal, friendly gesture considering he knew what was to come. Maybe he was thawing toward the idea of advertising this place? Yeah, and maybe she was ready to run naked through the resort lobby.

"That cliché flattery will get your everywhere?" She bumped him back, harder. "Don't believe it. Utter crap."

He laughed. "God, I love your bluntness."

"You'd be one of few," she said, remembering the many times her big mouth had gotten her into trouble.

At home with her folks when she'd had a gutful of the many years of her parents' dysfunctional marriage and had told them so. She'd called her mom a sniveling, spineless woman who needed to kick her dad's ass to the curb. And she'd called her dad a narcissistic, self-absorbed bastard for treating Mom the way he did. The result? Her mom had actually paid attention and got a life for a month or two; the same two months her dad actually made it home more often.

She'd been home from college at the time, and that was the one and only vacation she remembered as being halfway tolerable. But when the obligatory phone calls to her folks the following semester had garnered more of the same old, same old, she'd never returned home for a vacation again. She'd swapped tension-fraught Texas for laid-back LA, crashing at Allegra's for Thanksgiving, Christmas, and any other college vacations. And she'd become hooked on the city.

She'd had no qualms about using her trust fund money to establish AW Advertising after college, but she'd deliberately taken a lesser role despite Allegra bugging her for weeks to be partner. Simply, Zoe didn't think she'd earned it.

She'd partied her way through college, cramming for exams and barely scraping through with passing grades, while Allegra studied her brainiac ass off and received top honors. She'd gotten a marketing degree by pure chance— after throwing a dart at a course prospectus following a particularly wild tequila shot party—while it had been Allegra's dream for years.

Working behind the scenes suited her, because she'd never felt worthy.

As for her most recent bout of bluntness, when the company's clients had labeled her ideas *too avant-garde, outrageous, and damaging* before taking their business elsewhere? Boy, did her mouth get her in trouble that day.

"You've gone quiet." He half turned toward her, resting his arm along the back of the bench. "Should I be worried?"

"Absolutely." She pointed at the empty beach in front of them. "It's a sin that a place as gorgeous as this isn't on the tourist map. And did you notice the lack of resort guests as we strolled through the grounds?"

"I noticed." By his casual shrug, he didn't seem all that concerned. "Expanding this place will only create rooms that won't be filled."

"They'll be filled all right, and you know it." She made a picture frame with her hands and panned it left to right, encompassing the resort's sole pool, the beach, and the barbecue/bar area. "Kaluna's given AW Advertising a massive budget to ensure worldwide coverage of this place, and we stand by our work."

"So you can give me a guarantee?"

Annoyed by his baiting her, she lowered her arms. "You know there are no guarantees in business, but I can tell you this. You're smart. You would've researched AW and seen what we've done with Kaluna's flagship Palm Bay resort and the new Whitsunday resort."

She swept her arm wide, to encompass the view. "With Kaluna's planned renovation and an update to the resort, AW Advertising will get the people here."

"You're that confident?"

She nodded. "I'm not in the habit of saying things I don't mean."

"In that case, tell me you can't wait to get back to the US and leave all this behind."

Confused, Zoe searched his face for answers. Answers she didn't like once the implication of what he'd asked hit her.

He'd trapped her. He wanted her to say she didn't want to leave. But why? Unless...

"Don't tell me." She clutched her heart in a mock swoon, resorting to flippant to handle what could be potentially dangerous admissions on both their parts. "You're going to miss me, and you want me to stay?"

"I didn't say that." He reached out and touched her shoulder, his fingertip trailing down her bare arm and leaving a trail of goose bumps in its wake.

"Because you wanted *me* to say it," she said, swatting away his hand. "Coward."

"Name-calling won't get me to agree to your proposal."

"Then what will?" She showed him her palms, nothing to hide. "I'll be honest here, Dom. I'm done. You've seen what I have to offer on behalf of AW. We can do great things together. But your evasiveness is starting to worry me."

And piss her off, but she wisely kept that gem to herself. There was only so far her bluntness would take her.

"Let me think about it, and I'll give you my answer tomorrow, when we return to Osturo."

Zoe had to be happy with that. It was the first time he'd acknowledged he'd even consider her proposal, so it was a win. The fact she had to wait another day for his answer? Considering it would be their final twenty-four hours together, and they'd be on a stunning island... well, maybe it wasn't all bad.

"Why are we staying 'til tomorrow?"

"Because some things can't be rushed."

She had no idea what he meant, but the way he was staring at her? Made her supremely uncomfortable. He looked like a guy as out of his league as she was.

Lord help them both.

Zoe didn't believe in romance. Trumped-up bullshit that some guys used to get what they ultimately wanted. Sex. But considering Dom had already scored in that regard, she had no idea why he'd gone to all this trouble.

He'd organized some grand surprise for her apparently, and it had to be by moonlight. She shouldn't be this excited, but she was. Not many people did nice stuff for her. She didn't let them, preferring to take the short and sweet approach to everything in her life. So being indulged by a sexy prince on her last night on Ancora? She'd go with it for now.

"Keep your eyes closed, we're almost there," he said, holding her hand tight as he led her along a rough path. "And no peeking."

"You know if I fall and break my ankle, I'm going to sue, right?"

"I won't let anything happen to you," he said, his breath fanning her ear, and damned if she didn't believe him.

Dom was that kind of guy: Upstanding. Responsible. Caring. He'd make a great boyfriend. Husband, too. Something his dumbass fiancée obviously hadn't realized. It wasn't nice to think ill of the dead, but Zoe hadn't known the woman, so it didn't count.

"That's what they all say," she said, stumbling a little on purpose.

His arm instantly slid around her waist, anchoring her securely to his side. Hmm...maybe there were benefits to being a helpless female after all.

"Haven't you had a guy look after you before?"

"I don't need looking after," she said, wondering when her usual independent spiel had become so tired and old.

For the longest time, she hadn't wanted a long-term relationship. As for marriage, she'd never wanted to participate in the whole "initial grand passion fading to like and ultimately dislike" that it entailed. She'd attributed her apathy over the years to her parents' warped marriage, but it was more than that.

She just couldn't imagine loving one guy enough to want to be tied to him for life.

She'd been in love a few times: college infatuations mostly, which had fizzled out. But nothing earth-shattering. And never anything that lasted beyond a few months. Her breakups had been swift and clean. Which signaled that she'd never been fully emotionally invested in the first place.

It hadn't bothered her, and as the years had passed, while girlfriends settled down to domestic bliss and babies, she continued to live life on her terms: fast and furious. It suited her.

Until that last one-night stand when *she'd* taken a stand. When a badass like her bawled after having reasonably good sex resulting in orgasm, there had to be something wrong. Maybe she'd had one too many casual encounters. Maybe she kept hanging out with the wrong kind of guy. But whatever had snapped inside her that night, she'd taken it as a sign to change.

She wasn't on the lookout for a husband; far from it. She'd just wanted to take a break from the meaningless one-nighters and focus on doing a kick-ass job for AW. A plan that had been working fine, until she'd met Dom.

"You don't believe in marriage?"

"I've never met anyone worth loving enough to spend the rest of my life with."

The simple truth made her sound harsh and judgmental and picky. He'd probably think she was a heartless bitch. His opinion of her shouldn't matter, but it did. Stupid, considering she'd never see him again after tomorrow.

"I understand," he said, so softly she barely heard it. "It's important to have standards."

Great, now he was picturing her as some kind of saint. If he only knew. This saint's halo had slipped to her ankles a long time ago.

"It's also important to live life to the fullest, and that's what I've done." Did that sound as shallow to him as it did to her?

"But now?"

Trust Mr. Intuitive to home in on what she hadn't said rather than what she'd said.

"Now I'm looking for something more." Uh-oh. Where the hell had *that* come from?

He didn't respond, but she could hear his soft breathing in the night silence, as she silently cursed for opening up like that.

She could blame the surrealism of the situation, but she knew better. Dom was easy to talk to. He was a good listener who seemed genuinely interested in her and who asked the right questions. If she were ever foolish enough to give her heart to any guy, she'd want someone like him.

"Open your eyes," he said, his arm tightening around her waist.

Her eyelids fluttered open, and she gasped.

The scene before her was like something out of a romantic movie:

a private, natural lagoon fringed by a lemon grove, moonlight glinting off the water's surface, with a picnic laid out on the water's edge. Tea light candles rimmed the picnic blanket, their flames flickering softly on the still night.

"Do you like it?"

Zoe couldn't breathe. And her damn eyes burned with the sting of unshed tears.

This was too thoughtful, too nice, too much.

"It's beautiful," she said, not surprised when her voice quavered. "Thank you."

As if sensing how overwhelmed she was, he didn't say anything more and led her to the blanket. Before she could sit, he captured her face in his hands.

"We may have come together in the oddest of ways, but I wanted tonight to be about us. About enjoying each other's company. No expectations. No regrets."

The perfect speech to go with the perfect picnic. So why did Zoe have more than her fair share of regrets now that their time together was coming to an end? And those damn regrets had nothing to do with business.

"No regrets," she echoed, a second before his lips brushed hers in a soft butterfly kiss that melted her heart.

She wanted to deepen the kiss, wanted to obliterate the uncharacteristic glut of feelings clogging her chest, with wild good-bye sex. But Dom eased away, staring at her with questions she couldn't answer in his eyes.

"Do you want to eat or swim first?"

"But I didn't bring a swimsuit...oh."

At last, they were on the same page. A girl could get swept away by the romance of an evening like this, but the faster she grounded herself in sex, the better. No point getting used to this. They were worlds apart in so many ways, and Zoe the realist trumped Zoe the newly awakened closet romantic any day.

"What's wrong?" And just like that, he homed in how uncomfortable she was in this scenario.

"I'm a tad overwhelmed." She answered honestly, rather than coating her response in a cloak of deceit.

"By a little romance?"

"Uh-huh." She sank onto the blanket, tucked her knees up, and wrapped her arms around them. Classic defensive posture, but if he reached for her again, she may just blubber. "Look at me. I'm a spiky-haired bigmouth who barrels through life without taking time to smell the roses."

He snapped his fingers and winked. "Damn. Forgot the roses."

She smiled through her tears. "I'm not sure if it's all this or the fact that we're leaving the island tomorrow or I'm just growing sentimental in my old age, but I'm feeling a little fragile."

"Can't imagine a tough girl like you crying," he said, squeezing one of her biceps, trying to make her laugh.

To her absolute horror, she burst into tears.

"Hey, come here." He tried to bundle her into his arms, and she resisted for all of two seconds before giving in to the luxury of being held.

Unfortunately, once she started she couldn't stop. That's the thing about crying. Because she rarely cried, when she did, it was ugly. Real ugly. Great, snot-clogging sobs that made her body shake as she buried her head deeper into his chest.

He let her cry, smoothing her hair, her back. He didn't make stupid *ssh* sounds or mutter trite words. Instead, his silent comfort eventually seeped into her weary soul, and the tears dried up. And with it came the reality that she'd now have to answer the hard questions. Questions she could barely fathom, let alone devise a response for.

Because deep down, Zoe knew why she'd just made a fool of herself.

Despite all the logical reasons why she shouldn't fall for a guy like Dom, she already had.

In less than a week, she'd developed feelings for a guy as unobtainable as her being crowned Miss Universe. And it hurt. Hurt like a bitch that she'd have to walk away from him, from this, all too soon.

She placed her palms on his chest and pushed, grateful when he released her. "Don't look at me."

She held her hands over her face. Yeah, like that would be an improvement on the blotchy red skin and puffy bloodshot eyes.

"You're asking the impossible." He gently lowered her hands, not letting go. "I can't not look at you."

And damn if her heart didn't twang again.

"It's okay to express emotions," he said, his lips brushing soft kisses across her knuckles. "Even for a toughie like you."

She managed a wan smile. "Guess you can tell I don't cry very often."

"You're happy with your life. That's a good thing," he said, squeezing her hands before releasing them in order to uncork a bottle of Chianti.

"People cry tears of joy, too." She accepted a filled glass from him. "Maybe I don't have enough to be happy about?"

"In that case, let's make a toast." He tapped his glass against hers. "For the time we have left together, let's be happy."

"I'll drink to that." She downed the robust wine in five gulps, needing the alcohol hit to shock her out of this emotional overload.

"Hey, slow down. That's powerful stuff."

She pointed at his half-filled glass. "Then you should drink faster, so I can take advantage of you."

Rather than firing back a flirty quip as she expected, he lowered his glass and placed it on the picnic basket tray. "You do that a lot, don't you?"

Confused, she said, "Drink?"

"Try to deflect your feelings by focusing on sex."

Yowza. How did he do that? He barely knew her, yet he was more intuitive than most people in her life.

"You said we should be happy, and sex with you makes me

happy," she said, forcing a provocative smile and hoping he'd buy her deflection. "What's wrong with that?"

She waited an eternity for his answer, before he finally nodded. "Nothing. Absolutely nothing."

He plucked the empty wineglass out of her hands and placed it next to his. "Time for a swim."

Relieved he hadn't pushed her for answers she'd rather not give, Zoe allowed Dom to tug her to her feet, his solemn gaze never leaving hers. His arm slid around her waist, anchoring her, while his other hand slid up her back to snag the tag on her zipper. With infinite slowness he lowered it, the rasping of metal teeth the only sound mingling with her quickened breathing.

When her back was bared to the warm night air, his hands molded to her waist and moved upward, tugging down the straps holding her dress up. The cool cotton slithered down her body and pooled at her bare feet, leaving her naked bar a white satin thong.

"Perfect," he murmured, stepping back to admire her in the pale moonlight. "You're the most perfect woman I've ever met."

Zoe knew Dom was caught up in the romance of the moment, and a horny guy about to get laid would say anything. But for one heart-rending moment, she wished she could believe him.

"This is perfection." She splayed her palms across his chest, savoring the heat beneath the linen. She skimmed over every delicious muscle, the hardness so tempting.

Her fingers fumbled in her haste to unbutton him, and when the last button slid through the hole, she pushed the shirt off his broad shoulders, leaving him gloriously bare-chested.

Moonlight dappled his chest, highlighting the hard planes, the dips and ridges, the smoothness of skin. Gorgeous. She leaned forward and captured a nipple between her teeth, nipping it hard.

He groaned and pulled her toward him, claiming her mouth in an explosive kiss that snatched her breath and made her cling to him.

His firm fingers kneaded her ass before he slipped a finger beneath her thong and tugged, making it rub against her clit.

He swallowed her moan, his tongue taunting her as he ripped the thong clear off and lowered her to the blanket. She had no idea if it was the goose liver pâté or the eggplant dip digging into her back, but she solved the problem by rolling onto her side.

As he ravaged her mouth, he unzipped and sheathed himself. He nudged at her entrance, and in a smooth move, she rolled on top of him so that he entered her.

She tore her lips from his to sit up, bracing her hands on his chest.

And in that moment, looking down on Dom, their bodies straining to reach orgasm, their gazes locked in wide-eyed wonder at how damn explosive they were together every single time, Zoe finally admitted the truth.

Despite all self-talk to the contrary the last few days, despite all the years' worth of self-preservation from emotional attachment, she may have just fallen in love.

Chapter Fourteen

Dom couldn't tear his eyes off Zoe.

Was this even real? Having her straddling him outdoors, moonlight framing her, flickering candlelight casting alluring shadows over her breasts?

Like a fantasy come to life. But at least for tonight, she was all real, and she was all his.

He'd wanted to make tonight special for her, to make up for some of his previous behavior. He'd expected her to lap up the romance. He hadn't expected the tears. Seeing her so upset had gutted him in a way that made him reevaluate exactly how invested he was in this transient fling.

Fuck, he was in so much trouble.

He had to do his best to reassert what this was about: two people who shared a powerful sexual connection.

He thrust upward, delighting in her gasp. So he did it again and again, until they were both mindless.

She rode him with the same exuberance she had for life: wild and unrestrained. Bringing them to the brink hard and fast.

And just when he thought it couldn't get any better, she touched herself. Fingering her clit to accelerate her orgasm.

His balls tightened in anticipation a second before he shot his load, the power of his orgasm making his head feel like it was clamped in a vise.

She threw back her head a second later, her cries of release echoing in the silence.

He would never forget this image as long as he lived: his hedonistic woman in the throes of passion.

Back arched. Breasts thrust to the night sky. The elegant column of her neck.

She was magnificent.

And he wished she was all his.

All too soon, she straightened and slid off. For some inexplicable reason, she wouldn't look at him, and it irked. They'd just shared what was a monumentally special moment for him...didn't she feel anything? Or was she feeling as overwhelmed as he was and didn't want to risk another crying jag?

He needed to get this back onto familiar territory. The two of them sparring. Lighthearted. Fun. No commitment.

The way his chest ached at the thought? Yep, he was totally, 100 percent fucked.

"How about that swim now?" He turned away and took care of business. "The water's perfect."

"Sounds good." She whacked him on the ass with a playful slap. "I like the idea of skinny-dipping with a prince."

"Why? So you get bragging rights back home?"

She stepped around him, her bold stare deliberately lingering on his cock. "And my, my, isn't there a lot to brag about."

He laughed. "You've already had your wicked way with me, so no need to lay the flattery on thick."

"Ah, but there is." She stepped in close, cupped him. "Because after our swim? I'm hoping for round two."

"You've got yourself a deal."

She squeezed him in response, and he lunged for her. But she was too quick. Dodging. Weaving. Making a beeline for the water, where she executed a cute little ass-wiggling dive into the lagoon.

Dom added that snapshot to the many he'd stored away in his memory.

For when Zoe left, he had a feeling his life would be more bereft than ever.

Chapter Fifteen

Dom had been determined to keep their final hour on the island lighthearted.

He wanted Zoe to remember this place as he did: filled with warmth and humor and magic.

So he'd brought her to his special place—the waterfall— to say good-bye.

Big mistake. Huge. Because now that they were here, he was in dire danger of saying something he'd regret. Something like "stay with me."

"This was my hideout as a kid," he said, taking hold of her hand as they stood before the tumbling waterfall that gushed and burbled. "When I was here, the rest of the world didn't exist."

"It's beautiful," she said, with the right amount of reverence. She got him. She really did. And he couldn't say that about many people in this world. "But if you're hoping for a repeat of last night's water seduction, we don't have time." She elbowed him and winked. "Though maybe if you're really quick..."

He smiled and tugged on her hand, bringing her into the circle of his arms. "I've never brought anyone here before."

He wanted her to realize how special this was. Hell, he wanted her to read his mind. But what would that tell her?

That he was a mess, trying to sort through a confused jumble of thoughts?

That he was seriously thinking of compromising the oath he'd made to himself to honor his father's memory, because he wanted to keep her with him longer and thought he could achieve that by agreeing to work with her?

That he was going stark, raving mad at the thought of losing her?

"Bet you say that to all the girls." She winked, her signature cheekiness one of the many things he'd miss about her.

"You're the only one," he said, wondering if the gravity of his declaration would register.

He meant it. She was the only one. The only woman he'd ever let get this close emotionally. And it terrified him.

Against his better judgment, he'd grown to trust Zoe. Hell, even his grandmother trusted her, and that was a far cry from Nonna's feelings for Lilia.

But what if his lust for her was jumbled up with the rest of his feelings, and making him go a little nuts?

He never went out on a limb with anyone for fear of being left alone regardless when they didn't get what they wanted. What made him think Zoe would be any different?

"Careful there, Your Highness. That almost sounded like you've enjoyed having me around."

"Maybe a little?" He held up his hand, wavered it from side to side, reverting to flippant when she'd just given him the perfect opportunity to say how he was really feeling. *Testa di cazzo.* "You've turned out okay for a crazed kidnapper."

"And you were the perfect hostage." She stood on tiptoes to kiss him, an all-too-brief brush of her lips on his.

"Damn shame I have to release you."

Now it was his turn to wonder if she meant that or not, but he never got the chance to ask when she laughed and slipped out of his embrace.

"Come on, let's go. I'm overdue for a videoconference with my partner at AW."

So it was back to business as usual. He should be glad they were reestablishing boundaries that would only get more constricted when they reached Osturo.

But here, now, for a suspended moment in time, Dominic wished he were an ordinary guy without a title, without the burden of his heritage and the promises he'd made bearing down on him.

Because he'd like nothing better than to throw caution to the wind for the first time in his life and follow Zoe to the ends of the earth.

...

The moment Zoe entered the castle, some of the residual tension pinching her shoulders eased.

Until now, her spine had felt stiff, like she'd been walking around with a stick up her ass all day. Yeah, she'd been that tense. From the moment she opened her eyes this morning to five minutes ago, when Dom had left her to go in search of his grandmother, Zoe had been uptight and edgy.

Last night had solidified what she'd suspected for a few days. She'd fallen in love with a prince, and there wasn't one damn thing she could do about it except leave.

The crazy thing was, she thought Dom may return her feelings. And despite the incredible night they'd shared last night, first by the lagoon and later in his bed, they'd skirted around the main issues this morning. Hinting at more but neither having the balls to say...*where to from here?*

WANTON HEAT

They'd been so close at the waterfall this morning. She wasn't a complete fool. She understood the significance of him pointing out she was the only woman he'd taken there.

She'd wanted to push him for answers, had wanted him to articulate if he was feeling half of what she was. But she hadn't pushed, for fear of what that may mean. A frightening choice between her head and her heart.

And she'd be damned if she listened to her heart. Women made stupid decisions based on their impressionable hearts. Now that she'd fallen in love, she understood why. Love turned logic to mush and fueled futile fantasies, the main one being her staying with Dom if he asked her.

What was worse? The surreal romance of the last twenty-four hours had pushed business to the back of her mind when it should be at the forefront. She couldn't afford to mess this up, but what if after all this, Dom still said no?

Not once during their time together had the business/ pleasure lines blurred. When she'd been in his arms, she'd been totally in the moment, not considering business at all. But now that they'd returned, and he'd said he'd give her his answer today, the enormity of the situation hit.

Would she have the guts to walk away if Dom said no?

Business-wise, she should stay and fight for what she wanted.

Personally, if she spent any more one-on-one time with him, she may just blurt the truth, and that wouldn't help either of them.

Damn, she was in a bind. Of her own making.

"My grandson is happier than I've seen in ages, and I have you to thank for that." Catarina breezed into the room, her expression serene.

By looking at the regal older woman, Zoe never would've guessed a Machiavellian mastermind resided in that scheming brain.

"You knew that storm would keep us stranded for days." It was a statement, not a question, and to Catarina's credit, she nodded immediately.

"Of course."

"And you wanted us stranded together for that long because...?"

"I think the glows you're both sporting is answer enough." Catarina sat on an ivory armchair and rested her hands in her lap. "I saw instantly you sparked something in my grandson. That morning you arrived? He appeared more alive than he has in years." She shrugged. "So I played matchmaker and pushed you two together for a while? No harm done."

Zoe wanted to tell the queen she was wrong. A huge injustice had been done, because what the monarch saw as a short-term solution to her grandson's unhappiness had resulted in potentially breaking Zoe's heart.

Why was it, when she'd finally decided to shed her old ways and look for a committed relationship with one guy, that he had to be out of reach?

"You, my dear, look radiant," Catarina said, pride in her scheme audible. "And Dominic is positively beaming."

Catarina paused, tilted her head to one side, studying her. "After hearing your entire presentation, has he agreed to your terms?"

"Not yet." Zoe shook her head. "He's giving me his final answer today."

"Interesting." Catarina's gnarled fingers drummed against her thigh. "If he hasn't said an outright no, you may just have succeeded in your quest to change one stubborn man's mind."

"I hope so." Because the reality was, Zoe wasn't so sure. She'd done the unthinkable and let hormones cloud her judgment. Because if she hadn't had sex with Dom, hadn't fallen for him, she probably would've kept badgering him for an answer. She would've hassled him and harangued him 24-7 until he'd given her an answer just to get her to shut the hell up. She would've stayed focused on the ultimate goal, instead of letting him sweep her off her feet.

"This is none of my business, but do you have feelings for my grandson?"

Startled by Catarina's bluntness, Zoe tried to school her face into a blank mask, but by the knowing glint in the older woman's eyes, it was too late.

"I thought so." Catarina nodded, surprisingly smug. "Well, then, you've both got more than a business proposition to figure out."

"There's nothing to figure out," Zoe blurted, unnerved by Catarina's perception. "My life is in LA. Dom's is here. We're from different classes. We have absolutely nothing in common."

"And yet you fell in love with him in less than a week," Catarina said, annoyingly calm. "I think that says a lot."

"You're wrong," Zoe said, her empty protest sounding too loud in the cavernous room.

It was bad enough she'd bought into the ridiculous romantic fantasy she'd concocted in her head; having the queen articulate it like it was fact didn't help.

"Am I?" Catarina stood and to Zoe's shock, bent to kiss her on the cheek. "There are no class distinctions on these islands. The monarchy is but an ancient title. As you know, my grandson is a modern businessman who makes calculated decisions." She straightened and bestowed a kind smile. "I'm hoping he makes a wise decision when it comes to you."

Zoe tried to convince herself Catarina meant in the business arena, but they both knew differently.

Zoe didn't dare hope there was a chance for her and Dom, but for a wishful second, it sure was nice to dream.

When Catarina left the room, Zoe fired up her tablet to videoconference Allegra. With the time differences between here and Australia, it should be late evening Down Under. What Zoe needed right now was Allegra's cool logic. A voice of reason. Anything to distract from the nerves making her hands shake.

She needed Dom to agree to her business proposal. As for anything else? Didn't bear thinking about.

Allegra's face popped onto the screen, her eyes a little unfocused. "Hey Zo-Zo, how's it going?"

Zoe grimaced. "Oh my God, look at your eyes. I've interrupted another sex-athon."

Allegra grinned, the grin of a well-satisfied woman. "Don't worry about it. Jett's making me a hot chocolate while we chat."

"You've got him under this already." Zoe pressed a thumb to her forehead. "Lucky bitch."

Allegra chuckled. "Have to say, I never in a million years dreamed I'd be this happy."

While Zoe was pleased for her BFF, she couldn't help the small sliver of jealousy that wounded her already fragile heart. "You deserve it, babe."

"I do, don't I?" Allegra squared her shoulders, a woman confident in the love of her man. "So do you have a verdict on the ad campaign yet?"

"No, but I should know shortly."

"That arrogant prince holding out on you?" Allegra didn't know the half of it.

"About that...has Kaluna considered other alternatives to expanding the resort? Because now that I've had the grand tour of Ancora, I can understand where Dom's coming from."

And she'd gone as far as to jot down a few alternative ideas that could meld both their visions if he were enlightened enough.

Allegra frowned. "Dom?"

Damn, Zoe had just tipped her hand. She'd wanted to put out a few feelers to see if there was a way that Dom would get his way, and she would get hers. A compromise. Instead, she'd just alerted her friend that what she shared with the prince had moved way beyond business.

"Don't tell me you slept with him?" Allegra shook her head.

"Fine. I won't tell you then." Zoe tried to sound upbeat, when in fact she knew she'd screwed up by screwing Dom.

Allegra waggled a finger at the screen. "What were you thinking?"

"Probably the same thing you were when you *slept with* Jett on

Palm Bay." Zoe tapped her bottom lip, pretending to ponder. "Because as I recall, technically he was business, too, but that didn't stop you."

"Touché." Allegra's wry grin made Zoe laugh. "But royalty? Seriously?"

"You can call me Princess," Zoe said, faking a bow.

Allegra's smile faded. "Zo-Zo, this is serious. You know we can't muck up Kaluna's worldwide advertising campaign."

"Believe me, I know," Zoe said, well aware there was more on the line than Kaluna's campaign. Their entire company depended on scoring this gig.

The sly glint in Allegra's curious gaze alerted Zoe to the incoming question as her friend leaned closer to the screen. "So how was he?"

"Unbe-fricking-lievable." Zoe mock swiped her brow. "And that's an understatement."

"Wow," Allegra mouthed. "That good?" "Better."

Allegra hesitated, and gnawed on her bottom lip, as if holding back.

"What?" Zoe prompted.

Allegra sighed and pinched the bridge of her nose. "It's just that before you left, you said you weren't doing the fling thing anymore. That you were taking a break from the casual lifestyle."

Zoe bit back her first response of "maybe I found something more," and the silence stretched to uncomfortable. Allegra stared at her with concern.

"Oh, no, hon, you've fallen for him? But he's an Italian prince. And you're..."

Stung by what her friend hadn't said rather than by what she had, Zoe squared her shoulders. "I'm what? Too common? Trashy? Flamboyant?"

Sadness downturned Allegra's mouth. "I was going to say you're an LA girl through and through. Your whole life is there. And you've just been made partner at AW. How could you give all that up?"

"I couldn't," Zoe said, but the lie sounded hollow even to her ears. "But splitting your time between LA and Australia seems to be working for you."

Allegra glanced away guiltily. "But that's partially for work—"

"Bullshit. Even if Jett wasn't working on the Whitsunday Kaluna campaign, you'd be spending every spare minute you had in Oz."

Allegra hesitated, before continuing. "Has he said anything? I mean, are you two seriously considering trying a relationship?" She pressed her hands to her cheeks and didn't wait for an answer. "A prince, Zo-Zo? Oh my God. This is so surreal."

"I know," Zoe said, knowing she couldn't have kept something like this from her BFF but wishing Allegra didn't sound so incredulous.

Mismatched couples made it all the time. Beauty and the Beast. Cinderella and her prince. Pretty crappy that the only successful relationships she could come up with were fictional fairy tales. "But we haven't discussed anything, and if all goes well, I'll get the go-ahead for our ad campaign soon, and I'll be on the ferry back to the mainland this afternoon."

"That's it?"

"What do you mean?"

"You're not going to try and make a go of it?"

Zoe was many things, a realist being top of the list. "You said it yourself. I've got too much happening back in LA. And ultimately, our differences would drive us apart."

Allegra pouted. "I wish things could work out for you."

"Me too, babe, me too." Zoe made a grand show of glancing at her watch. "Anyway, I gotta go. I'm meeting Dom shortly."

"Okay." Allegra kissed her fingertips and pressed them to the screen. "Take care, hon. And I'm here if you need me for anything, day or night."

"Thanks." Zoe blew a kiss at the screen. "Talk soon."

She ended the call before the emotion welling in her chest spilled forth. While she'd videoconferenced Allegra to keep her abreast of business developments, having her friend learn the truth about her relationship with Dom had made it more real somehow.

As long as they were the only two people involved, it had been okay to dismiss it as a romantic fantasy. But first Catarina gave her blessing, and now Allegra.

Zoe didn't believe in false hope, but for one wistful second, she wished she did.

Chapter Sixteen

Dominic surveyed his desk, a scotch in one hand, Zoe's ad campaign in the other.

He knew coming back to Osturo would ground him. Would get him back on track. Focused.

Three things he hadn't been on Ancora with Zoe.

Zoe.

She waited for him downstairs. Waited for his answer to her proposal. And for the first time since he'd envisaged preserving these islands to honor his father's memory, he wavered.

Her kick-ass presentation and her vision for the region had gotten to him. She was as passionate about her business as she was in the bedroom. That kind of passion captivated him. She captivated him.

But was it all a ruse?

He sank into his leather executive chair and downed the scotch. It burned his gullet, but not half as much as the same old doubts plaguing him.

He'd been a fool once before, being blinded to reality by lust for a woman. Lilia had playacted the role of devoted fiancée while brokering a deal with his biggest rival.

Was Zoe doing the same? Pretending to have feelings for him to get what she wanted?

He'd like to think he'd wised up since his engagement debacle, but his feelings for Zoe had addled his brain. Was her part in their mutual seduction merely an act?

Having his agreement for the Kaluna worldwide ad campaign meant everything to her. How far would she go to get it?

Yet her tears last night belied any deception. The depth of emotion she'd shown had shocked him, especially from one who was so bold usually. He could've pushed her for answers, but he'd been afraid. What if she'd given the answer he feared the most? That she felt more for him than was good for either of them.

Because if Zoe reciprocated his feelings...what did that mean? That they actually had a chance at making a relationship work or had he been too closed off emotionally for too many years to assess the situation objectively: that Zoe was just like the rest, doing whatever it took to get what she wanted from him?

"Fuck," he muttered, slamming the empty scotch glass onto the desk and firing up his PC.

He'd been offline for four days, and while he wasn't expecting anything requiring his urgent attention, he was hopeful the PI had come through with some information that may make his decision easier.

Besides, he needed to buy more time before his confrontation with Zoe.

He wanted to say no to her proposal. He wanted her to say yes to his.

He was so screwed.

Scrolling through his in-box, he mentally recited what he could possibly say to convince her to stay. Other than the startling truth.

I think I'm in love with you.

An e-mail with the subject header "KALUNA RESORT EXPANSION" caught his eye. At last. Information from the PI.

Dominic clicked it open and read, every word driving a dagger into his heart.

Kaluna had found a loophole in the contract and had already obtained the necessary permits to move forward with expanding his resort. A larger, shinier, newer resort that would bring in more tourists regardless if Dominic signed off on an ad campaign or not.

Which meant Zoe had been playing him for a fool.

She'd been softening him up for a fait accompli.

Dominic reread the e-mail, twice, just to make sure he hadn't misunderstood. Only then did he allow his slow-burning anger to spread, filling him with a rage that made him shake.

He wanted to smash his fist through the PC screen. He wanted to pick up his scotch glass and fling it against the wall.

Instead, he stalked around the desk and headed for the door, intent on confronting the woman he'd let into his bruised heart, the woman who'd shattered it once and for all.

...

Zoe's heart gave a betraying leap as Dom strode into the ground-floor library.

He'd changed into a black suit, pale-blue shirt, and amethyst tie. A stylish combination that transformed him from gorgeous to knock-out. Though it wasn't the suit that impressed her as much as the guy in it. If her memory served correct, he'd looked pretty damned incredible naked, too.

She couldn't suppress a coy smile, wondering if he could read her mind. However, when her gaze met his, her smile faltered.

Something was wrong. Drastically wrong, if the fury radiating off him like a nuclear cloud was any indication.

"What's up?" She stood and moved toward him.

He paused in the doorway as if ready for flight. When she got close enough, she saw she'd underestimated the extent of his anger. He wasn't furious. He was rigid with rage.

"Don't." He held up his hands and she stopped a few feet away. "I've had enough."

Foreboding made her wrap her arms around her middle. "I don't understand—"

"Like hell you don't."

She flinched as he spat the icy words.

"You *knew* what honesty meant to me." He jabbed a finger at her. "You knew what I'd been through with Lilia's betrayal."

He lowered his hand, his fingers curling into his palm to form a fist. "*Dio*, you must've thought I was a gullible idiot, falling for your act."

Zoe started to shake. She had no idea what Dom was talking about, but he obviously blamed her for something. Something big. And she didn't know what pissed her off more: the fact that he hadn't had the decency to ask her about it first or the fact that the guy she loved thought so little of her.

"What is it I'm supposed to have done?"

"You're still acting? Even now?" he roared, slamming the door shut with his fist. "You know the worst part? I was actually considering that we could work together in some capacity. That you would understand if I told you the truth. Instead, you deceived me."

As Zoe's confusion receded, indignation took its place. "Stop right there and tell me what exactly I'm supposed to have done."

His laser-like glare sliced her in two. "Permits have been granted. The Kaluna expansion is going ahead."

"But that's not possible..."

She'd just spoken to Allegra, and they would've known about it considering it impacted the ad campaign.

"So what were you? A diversion to keep me occupied while the deal went through behind my back?" His gaze deliberately perused her body in a pure insult. "There's a name for women who use their bodies for—"

"Shut the fuck up." She was in his face in two seconds flat, palms against his chest, shoving him, hard. "Don't you dare make vile insinuations when I had nothing to do with this." She pushed him again. "And what you're implying? It's insulting and sickening."

She whirled away, annoyed by the angry sting of tears. "But it's nice to know what you really think of me, you bastard."

"You're calling me names after what you've done?"

She would've laughed at the outraged incredulity in his voice if it weren't for the fact that he'd just called her a lying whore.

Dragging in deep, calming breaths, she turned to face him. "I haven't *done* anything. I didn't know the permits had been granted; otherwise, I wouldn't have wasted my time devising a few plans of my own when we got back this morning. Plans that involved Kaluna leaving the expansion alone and you developing Osturo instead. And a kick-ass ad campaign to make both islands prosper."

God, she'd been such a fool, trying to work on a compromise that would ensure a win-win for them both. "As for what happened between you and me?"

She sneered, mustering every ounce of antagonism she could to eradicate the pain making her chest ache courtesy of his accusations. "I'm not some cheap hooker who sells her body for anything. But thanks for saying I am."

He stared at her, stony-faced, but she scored a direct hit with the hooker comment as regret clouded his eyes.

"And for the record? I don't give a flying fuck what you do with your hick islands anymore." She pointed out the window at the incredible view. "I'm going to hand over the resort campaign to some other sucker who'll waste their time trying to convince a stubborn dickhead like you what's good business sense."

Dom gaped as she strode past him and opened the door, desperate to escape before she went too far.

WANTON HEAT

She paused on the threshold. "And just so you know? The sex wasn't all that great."

She slammed the door and let the tears fall.

So much for not going too far.

Chapter Seventeen

Thirty minutes later, Dominic still couldn't comprehend how his life could've imploded so badly.

After Zoe had stormed out, he'd sat by the window and stared at the view without seeing it, going over the entire episode in his head.

If he'd been furious at the thought of being duped by her, she'd been livid following his accusations. He'd gone too far, implying she'd used her body to distract him. But he'd been so bloody angry, and her innocent act had pushed his buttons even more, that he'd wanted to hurt her as much as she'd hurt him.

He never should've gone that far though. She was right. He was a bastard. A dumb, stubborn bastard who had no idea what to do to make this right.

As for her admission that she wanted to leave Ancora alone and encourage development on Osturo? Proved that he'd made a huge mistake.

Zoe got it. She understood what preserving Ancora meant to him. And she'd tried to come up with a solution, despite her ad campaign's hinging on the expansion. She'd never sacrifice her goal unless she cared. A hell of a lot.

Fuck.

"Everything okay in here?" Catarina entered the library. "I heard raised voices half an hour ago, and now Zoe has taken her bags and headed into town to wait for the ferry."

"What?" He leaped to his feet, stung into action by the news Zoe had left. "When did she leave?"

"About ten minutes ago." Catarina glanced at her watch and nodded. "Which means you don't have long if you want to go after her and grovel."

"How do you know any of this is my fault?"

"Because I know you, Nicci Ricci," she said. "You're scared. Terrified, in fact, by your feelings for Zoe. So you've used whatever means possible to push her away."

She patted his cheek. "But you've pushed too hard this time, because Zoe is a headstrong woman who won't stand for any nonsense, least of all from the man she loves."

It took a moment for him to absorb Nonna's words, another to make sense of them.

"Zoe doesn't love me. She despises me."

The sex wasn't all that great still rung in his ears. Had he gotten it so wrong with Zoe, or had she being trying to wound him by aiming for his precious ego?

It hadn't mattered at the time, he'd been so angry. At her, for having the power to hurt him so badly. At himself, for opening himself up to a world of pain.

"You're smarter than that, Nicci." She pointed to his heart. "You know what's right, deep down in there. Trust your heart."

He had once before, and look where that had gotten him. Screwed over in the worst possible way. But he'd said it himself: Zoe was nothing like Lilia. And he wasn't some raw-boned youngster who resented a woman because he'd been burned in the past.

He'd been willing to give a relationship a chance before he'd seen that incriminating e-mail. Yet if he'd jumped to the wrong conclusions and falsely accused Zoe...Nonna was right. He had to chase after her and start groveling.

"Did Zoe say something to you?"

Catarina smiled, wisdom lines fanning from the corners of her eyes. "She didn't need to. Her feelings for you were written all over her face." She waggled her finger at him. "I'm old, but I'm not senile. I saw the way you two sparked when she first arrived."

"That's why you coerced her into kidnapping me before the big storm, because you knew we'd be stranded on Ancora for days?"

She tapped her temple. "Like I said, not senile yet."

Dominic slipped his arm around her bony waist and hugged. "So I take it you approve of Zoe?"

"She's the one for you."

Considering Nonna's track record with long-term relationship matches on the island, guess it was time he started believing her.

Catarina leaned into him, her slight frame reminding Dom of her physical fragility and advancing years despite her razor-sharp mind. "So what are you waiting for?"

"Thanks, Nonna." He kissed her cheek. "For everything."

She shooed him away. "You can thank me after you've convinced that poor girl you're not some moody lunatic."

He laughed. "I'll try."

But Dominic knew he'd have to do more than try. A hell of a lot more.

Chapter Eighteen

Zoe had to get off this frigging island before she went insane.

Apparently the afternoon ferry was delayed due to a problem with the engine, and she had two choices. Either sit on the dock and wait until the tugboat left or charter a private boat.

It was a no-brainer. She could charge it to the Kaluna expense account. Her visit to these godforsaken islands had been business. She'd been the dumbass to complicate the issue with pleasure.

The sex wasn't all that great.

Could she have told a more monumental lie? Sex with Dom had been phenomenal. And it would be one of the many things she'd have to forget about her stay.

Jeez, she'd messed up. Not only was the ad campaign in ruins without Dom's approval, but she may have single-handedly sunk AW Advertising for good.

What if Kai Kaluna thought the company was incompetent because *she* hadn't landed the Ancora ad campaign? What if he took his business and walked?

Crap.

This was her worst nightmare.

She'd failed. Again.

But this time was so much worse, because losing Kaluna would finish AW once and for all.

And she'd have to tell her BFF who'd always been there for her, that she was the one responsible for sinking their company.

Damn it.

Her fingers dug into her leather bag while she wished she could wrap them around Dom's neck and squeeze hard.

He'd hurt her. Badly. By not trusting her enough to give her the benefit of the doubt, by not caring about her enough to believe she'd never do something like that to him.

How had she gotten it so wrong? After their time together on Ancora, she'd thought…what? That he had feelings for her? That he may have fallen a little in love like she had?

Yeah, right. Looked like His Highness had been sowing his royal oats, and she'd been nothing more than a pleasant diversion while they'd been stranded.

She was such an *idiot* for believing otherwise.

The boat engine roared to life. Good. The sooner she got back to Naples, the sooner she could head home.

She'd read somewhere in her research that Ancora translated to light and Osturo to darkness. Wasn't that the truth? It was almost like Dom had been a different person on Ancora, his personality infused with a lightness she loved. On Osturo, he'd been a prick. And that's the guy she had to remember if she had any chance of forgetting him.

Water churned as the boat edged away from the dock and cruised toward open water. Zoe kept her gaze firmly on the receding shore. She wanted to memorize her last glimpse of Osturo and all it stood for. Pain. Heartache. Foolishness.

She'd deliberately chosen a seat at the stern for this purpose. Not because she wanted to look back, but because she needed to face her fears and prove she could do this anyway.

So she'd fallen in love and had her heart broken? Millions of rela-

WANTON HEAT

tionships shattered every day. And technically, she hadn't had a relationship to begin with.

She'd had a physical connection with a very sexy alpha prince. They'd had mind-blowing sex. That was it. End of story.

The sun's rays caressed her face, the comforting warmth making her eyelids droop. She was exhausted. Physically. Mentally. Emotionally. If only she could nap and awaken to find it had all been a nightmare.

She closed her eyes and tilted her face up to the sun. Maybe a little siesta between here and Naples wouldn't be out of the question…

Ten minutes later, the boat stopped, and her eyes snapped open.

Osturo was a long way behind and a quick glance port and starboard showed there was no land on either side.

Shit.

That's all she needed. For the boat to sink. Though drowning might be the easy way out considering how crappy her life was right now.

The boat bobbed like a cork as she made her way to the front. "Is there a problem…?"

"Depends on how you look at it," Dom said, emerging from the cabin. "If you want to hear me out and discuss this like two rational adults, there's no problem. If you don't, your only option is to jump overboard, in which case, that could be a distinct problem."

"What the hell are you doing?"

"Same thing you did." He had the audacity to grin. "Kidnapping you so I have a captive audience."

Secretly impressed by the lengths he'd gone to, she frowned and folded her arms. "Why don't you get your own material rather than copying mine?"

"Because yours worked so effectively, don't you think?"

The implication behind his words was clear, and she didn't need a reminder of how her kidnapping stunt had panned out.

"Well, your captive audience is right here." She stamped her foot for emphasis. "Though why you think I'd listen to a word you say is beyond me."

He gestured at the sea. "Because we're in the middle of the ocean, and you have no choice?"

"Smart-ass," she muttered. "I'll listen but doesn't mean I'll believe any of it after the shitty performance you put in at the castle."

He winced. "I'm sorry. I overreacted and said some heinous things."

"Heinous?" She snorted. "You can take the boy out of the castle, but you can't take the castle out of the boy."

"You're mocking me."

"Ten points to the guy with a crown on his head and a stick ten feet up his—"

"Be nice," he said, those mesmerizing lips she'd kissed so many times curving in amusement.

"Why? You weren't."

"Sulking doesn't become you," he said, pointing to the nearest bench seat. "Shall we sit and talk?"

"I guess." She shrugged, sounding every inch a recalcitrant kid, when in fact curiosity was eating away at her. He'd gone to great lengths to apologize. Which he'd just done. So what did they have to discuss?

"I want you to know I believe you," he said, waiting until she'd sat before doing the same. "I let my past cloud my judgment, and that was a stupid thing to do."

"It was." She nodded. "You should've asked me rather than flinging wild accusations."

"I should've done a lot of things..." He shook his head and stared straight ahead. "What happened on Ancora between us...the connection we shared...it unnerved me." He made circling motions at his temple. "Made me go a little crazy."

She knew the feeling, but she waited for him to continue.

"My recluse reputation isn't something I cultivated over the last few years. I've always been a loner by choice." He still didn't look at her, and she resisted the urge to hold his hand to encourage him to go on. "People always want something from me, and they'll stoop to any level to get it. So I learned to close myself off. To become unreachable emotionally. Then I turned to Lilia for comfort after my parents' death, and you know how that turned out."

He cleared his throat. "She was just using me, too. It's easier being alone. Being shut off. Not having to depend on anyone for anything, least of all to feel good about myself."

He finally swiveled his body to face her. "But that's how you make me feel. Happy. Like I'm truly alive for the first time in years."

He grimaced. "When I fucked everything up and thought I'd lost you?" He tapped his chest over his heart. "Hurt like a bitch in here."

His sincerity melted Zoe's resentment. He thought she'd betrayed him like Lilia had. But this didn't change anything. She needed a man to trust her, to believe in her enough that he wouldn't automatically assume the worst.

She'd vowed to never become like her mom, dependent on a guy for happiness. Yet that's exactly what she'd opened herself up for with Dominic.

The way he'd treated her? Had hurt more than she could've ever thought possible. She'd been shattered.

While she appreciated his apology, it didn't mean anything. Trite words to soothe his guilty conscience once he'd discovered the truth.

Ironic, that they both didn't let people get close, but for different reasons. The pain she was going through now when she'd only just fallen for him? Imagine how much worse it would be if she gave him her heart completely.

Not a chance in hell.

"And I don't want to lose you. Not ever again." He wound his fingers through hers and held on tight, while she attributed the queasiness in her stomach to the rocking boat. "I want you to stay with me, Zoe. What do you say?"

Zoe's fissured heart yelled a resounding yes.

Her head? Had just ruminated on every reason why she had to say no.

"I can't." She tried to slide her hand free but he tightened his grip. "My life is in LA—"

"The Kaluna ad campaign is yours," he blurted, the fear in his eyes beseeching her to understand. "And I'm well aware this will probably accelerate your departure. But I'm hoping..." He dragged in a breath and placed her hand over his heart, where it bucked like a wild thing. "I'm hoping you'll understand that I'm giving you this. My heart is yours."

Zoe swallowed, several times, unable to speak past the lump of emotion lodged in her throat.

Considering how he'd just revealed his innermost fears to her, that people only wanted him for what they could get, he'd virtually handed her his heart on a silver platter complete with carving knife.

Making a declaration like that, while expecting her to leave now that she'd gotten what she came for, was a bold move. She should know. She was prone to making brazen moves herself.

But considering the way he'd treated her before this, now wasn't one of those times.

"I appreciate your honesty, but I can't stay—"

"Your life can be here. You can work here. That idea you had, to develop Osturo and highlight both islands with an ad campaign?" He pinched the bridge of his nose and inhaled, and for a horrifying moment Zoe thought he might cry. "Shows me you get it. That you get *me*. I never wanted to change Ancora for personal reasons. But Kaluna found a loophole in the contract and is going ahead, so I need to make the best of a bad situation, and that means changing the way I think."

He released her hand, only to reach for her, but she sidled away. "I want to hear more about your ideas," he said.

So much for him giving her his heart. She hadn't said yes so he'd reverted to other means, appealing to her business sense. He made it sound so logical, but she wasn't a complete fool.

"So now you want to hear me out because you have no other option? Nice."

"It's not like that." He swiped a hand over his face. It did little to ease the tension furrowing his brows. "There's a reason I've been against expanding and promoting Ancora." He puffed out a breath. "My dad loved Ancora. He loved its wilderness. He pretended that Kaluna's resort didn't exist, so when he died, I made a promise to myself to preserve the island in his memory."

"That's noble," Zoe said, admiring his loyalty to his dad. "But surely he would've wanted this region to thrive?"

He shrugged. "Guess I've been reluctant to change anything on the islands for fear of letting him down in some way. Which sounds lame when I say it, but it's what I've believed in here for so long." He tapped his chest over his heart. "Thankfully Kaluna's new developer seems dedicated to preserving Ancora's wild beauty, so it's not all bad."

She nodded, increasingly touched by his devotion to his father.

"And if Ancora will be on the tourist map, it's time to develop Osturo, too, which is where you come in." His gentle smile made her heart twang. "Please tell me your ideas."

She could be an ass and tell him to stick it, but his honesty had gone some way toward soothing her wounded heart. "If Ancora is all about preserving its unspoiled beauty, I wanted to do the opposite with Osturo. Make it hip and happening. Provide a nice contrast for tourists coming to see the islands."

The appreciation in his eyes encouraged her to continue. "I thought it'd be cool to break with tradition and develop Osturo into the hot spot of the Mediterranean. A luxury resort, exclusive villas, restaurants, an open-air shopping marketplace, so people will want to visit and not only use it as a ferry stop to Ancora. With the bonus of providing new jobs and bringing in tourist dollars."

Zoe inadvertently held her breath, waiting for the verdict. Not that she cared what he did any more, considering she wouldn't be around, but she'd put a lot of thought into her plans.

For him.

Because she loved him.

A sentiment she needed to forget pronto.

Dom beamed, the kind of smile that hit Zoe in the solar plexus: swift and hard and damaging. And right then, she knew it would take her a long time to get over this man.

"You're amazing," he said, staring at her like she'd handed him a crown on a platter. "Absolutely brilliant."

Humbled by his praise, she nodded. "Good luck with it all—"

"But it'll mean nothing unless you devise a kick-ass ad campaign to put Osturo on the map." He held out his hand. "So what do you say? Fancy being my personal PR ad exec?"

Ironic, that in thinking she'd sunk AW Advertising, she had just landed the opportunity of a lifetime. Doing a personal campaign for Prince Dominic Ricci would ensure the company would have clients bashing down their door. And went a long way to assuaging her battered confidence after the debacle in LA, not to mention making amends with Allegra. Whom she could now tell the whole truth to.

But how could she work with Dom and keep things professional when she had to steel her heart?

"So let me get this straight. You're approving my ad campaign for Kaluna's resort on Ancora?"

He nodded. "But I want you to delegate Kaluna's campaign, so you work on my ad campaign only." His piercing blue gaze bore into hers. "You're exclusively mine."

For one fantastical moment, Zoe wished.

But she'd given up on wishes a long time ago, around the time her folks first separated before their inevitable tension-fraught reunions, and she learned there was no such thing as happily ever after.

"First you apologize, then you ask me to stay because I make you happy, then you change tack and couch your offer in business terms." She shook her head. "What the hell do you want from me?"

Zoe gritted her teeth to prevent saying any more. Was she really ready for an answer to that question?

He took an eternity to speak, his gaze never leaving hers. "I don't want anything from you." He raised one of her hands to his mouth and kissed it. "I just want you."

Zoe blinked. What was it about this guy that had a hard-ass chick like her on the verge of tears so often?

"I'm in love with you." He kissed the back of her other hand. "And I want a chance to explore a real relationship with you. Not just for a few days, but for longer."

When she didn't answer—difficult to speak past the lump of emotion clogging her throat—he continued. "Hopefully forever, if you'll have me."

Wow.

This was so not in her plans. But if there was one thing Zoe had learned over the years, it was that being a risk-taker could pay off.

"I don't believe in love," she said, and the hope in his eyes died. "My folks have a crappy marriage where my mom is dependent on my dad for happiness, and my dad doesn't give a shit about anyone but himself." She extricated her hands from his and this time he let her. "I've never had a real relationship. I think romance is for women desperate for validation and love is for schmucks."

She watched his expression morph from optimism to stone. "But you made me reevaluate every one of my preconceptions," she said, her voice soft and uncertain. "You, with your high and mighty assumptions that I'd fall at your feet. You, with your midnight lagoon picnics and private waterfalls and bedroom eyes."

She glanced away from the eyes in question, in case she drowned in them. "You made me fall in love with you, and damn it, there's not one sane reason why I should say yes to sticking around for you, but I will."

He let out an exultant whoop, stood, and hauled her into his arms, crushing her so hard she could barely breathe.

"Easy, big fella." She laughed, savoring the feel of being in his embrace again. "I'm not going anywhere."

"*Grazie, Dio*," he said, burying his face in the nook of her neck.

"I love it when you speak Italian," she said, loving him period.

"In that case, *ti voglio portare al letto e scoparti*," he murmured in her ear.

His husky tone indicated he'd said something naughty.

A girl could live in hope.

"What did you just say?"

"Let me take you below decks, and I'll show you." His exaggerated wink made her laugh.

She captured his face in her hands. "Are we really going to do this? Try a relationship? Work together?"

"With you by my side, there's nothing we can't do." His mouth crushed hers, his kiss obliterating the last of her doubts.

Zoe prided herself on not conforming.

Maybe it was time for the anarchist to become a monarchist after all...

Chapter Nineteen

"What time are we meeting your friends?" Dom slid his arms around her from behind as she applied a final slick of lip-gloss in front of the mirror and rested his chin on her shoulder. "Do we have time for a quickie?"

"God, you're insatiable." She wriggled her butt against his growing hard-on. "And no, we're due down in the lobby in two minutes."

He nipped the tender skin beneath her ear. "Which gives me sixty seconds to *abbassati gli slip*."

"Stop trying to sway me by saying wicked things with that sexy accent," she said, slapping his hand away as it zeroed in on the area that already throbbed for him. "But hold that thought for later."

"As you wish." He released her and slapped her butt playfully. "Taking your panties off will be but the start."

"Oh, baby, I wish." She cupped his hard-on, enjoying the flare of heat in his smoldering gaze. "I wish for you all the time."

"*Dio mio*, you drive me wild." He lunged for her, but she dodged, laughing.

"Come meet Allegra and Jett, and we can continue this discussion later."

He stalked toward her. "Trust me, *cara*, there'll be no talking when we get back here."

"Promises, promises," she flung over her shoulder as she opened the door before she changed her mind and ravaged him on the spot. Which wasn't entirely out of the question, considering they'd rarely made it out of the bedroom for the last week since she'd agree to stay.

When they weren't sexed up, they were busy poring over plans for Osturo and Zoe had to admit, the guy wasn't just a pretty face. There was a serious business brain behind the brawn and beauty. She was incredibly excited to be working with him on this. Opportunity of a lifetime. Now she had to convince her BFF and partner in AW that the only way she could do justice to a campaign of this magnitude was to stay on-site. Forever.

She'd been thrilled when Allegra said she'd be flying in to discuss the Kaluna campaign, because videoconferencing didn't cut it for the type of conversation they had to have.

Some of her misgivings must've shown on her face, because Dom slipped his hand into hers and squeezed. "It'll be okay. Your friend will understand."

"I hope so," Zoe said, glad she'd have Dom by her side when she broke the news, and relieved Allegra would have Jett to support her.

They strolled toward the lobby of Kaluna's resort, hand in hand, comfortable in their silence. That was another thing she loved about Dom—his ability to tune in to her many moods. She'd been independent too long to have a guy constantly demand attention, and thankfully, Dom wasn't like that. They were similar that way: content in their own company, not needing another person to complete them but appreciative to have someone alongside all the same.

"There they are." Zoe spotted her tall blond friend sitting alongside her handsome fiancé at a table for four on the outskirts of the veranda.

Dom squeezed her hand. "Ready?"

"As I'll ever be."

Feeling increasingly nervous the closer they got to the table, Zoe hoped to God Allegra would understand.

"Well, well, if it isn't my loved-up, suntanned BFF and her boy from Oz," Zoe said, bracing for Allegra's fierce hug as her friend squealed, leaped to her feet, and flung her arms around her.

"I've missed you so much, Zo-Zo." Allegra squeezed her tight, and Zoe said, "Ditto."

When they finally disengaged, the guys were shaking hands.

"So how're you treating my BFF, Aussie?" Zoe kissed Jett on the cheek.

"Like a princess," Jett said, his laconic drawl making her smile. "But I guess you'd know all about that?"

Zoe groaned and elbowed him, while Dom laughed.

"Allegra and Jett, I'd like you to meet Dom." Zoe nudged Allegra and said under her breath, "Don't forget to bow."

"Oh my God, really?" Allegra hesitated, her hand halfway out to shake Dom's, while the guys cracked up. "Pleased to meet you, Allegra." Dom shook Allegra's hand.

"Likewise." Her cool, confident friend almost simpered, and Zoe grinned.

Dom tended to have that effect on women, and it had nothing to do with his title. The guy looked like a photo enhanced Ian Somerhalder with the chiseled jaw and cheekbones, piercing blue eyes, and wicked smile. She was weak-kneed 24-7.

"Nice to see you've finally found your prince," Allegra said, keeping a straight face while delivering yet another pun.

Zoe groaned. "Are you two ever going to quit with the lame-ass royal puns?"

"No." Allegra and Jett shook their heads in unison.

Zoe turned to Dom. "Did you see that? Apparently getting engaged means you lose the ability to think independently and do everything in sync. How quaint."

Allegra slapped her forehead lightly. "Almost forgot. Check out the ring."

Instantly contrite, Zoe grabbed Allegra's left hand. She really must be gaga over Dom to forget something as important as her BFF's engagement ring. "Wow, babe, it's exquisite."

And it was. The stunning opal framed in diamonds was as unique as her friend.

Allegra clung to Jett's arm, gazing adoringly at her fiancé. "It's a black opal, the rarest of them all. And the second stunning Aussie thing in my life."

Zoe pretended to gag while Dom smiled benevolently. "Very romantic."

"Don't you go getting any ideas." Zoe jabbed Dom in the side with a finger.

"Wouldn't dream of it." Dom held his hands up in surrender. "I know how you feel about romance."

Allegra sniggered. "Is she still pulling that anti-romance crap? Because you know she's a marshmallow inside, really."

"Oh, I know." Dom slid an arm around her waist. "My little badass is as soft as whipped cream."

"You should know, considering you like me to spread it on your... ahem...and lick it off."

They all laughed as they sat at the table. Zoe's nerves had settled considerably with the banter that signified her relationship with Allegra. But now came the tough stuff.

"I've got something to tell you, and you're not going to like it," Zoe said, eyeballing Allegra. "You've been amazing in making me partner at AW recently, but there's a reason I accepted."

Allegra smiled. "Because it was way past time you stepped out of the shadows and into the limelight, babe."

Zoe gnawed on her bottom lip. "Trust me, I should've stayed in the shadows."

Confusion creased Allegra's brow and Zoe rushed on.

"Remember when you were on Palm Bay trying to land Kaluna, and I told you we lost our two oldest clients?"

Allegra nodded. "Uh-huh."

"I did that," Zoe said, heat flushing her cheeks in mortification. "I wanted to have a go at pitching on my own, so I devised a few new ideas and met with them." She winced. "Not only did they can my *outrageous* ideas, they said I was an upstart bigmouth, and they walked."

Allegra's eyes widened. "Why didn't you tell me?"

"Because I was ashamed. All my life people have sniggered behind my back that I'm nothing without Daddy's money, that I'm a nobody who didn't need to work, so I was desperate to prove myself."

Realization replaced Allegra's shocked expression. "That's why you insisted on being a PA all this time despite having an equal financial investment, isn't it?"

"Yeah. And considering I almost lost us the company, aren't you glad?"

"Idiot." Allegra slugged her on the arm. "You were right alongside me when we wowed Kaluna, so don't give me any of that self-defeating crap."

Zoe managed a wobbly grin. "There's something else."

Allegra rolled her eyes. "What now?"

Zoe glanced at Dom, who nodded, his silent support lending her courage. "I want out."

Allegra's jaw dropped. "But you've just scored the biggest coups for AW, doing the ad campaign for Kaluna's resort and for Dominic's redevelopment on Osturo. Why do you want to leave?"

"Because it's something I've been thinking about for a long time." Zoe sucked in a deep breath. "You're the face of AW, hon. It's your brainchild. I should never have accepted your offer of partnership. I only did it to make up for the way I screwed up in losing those clients."

Allegra's eyes narrowed. "Is this about the other employees?

Because they think you're taking advantage of our friendship and that's why you made partner?"

Zoe wavered her hand side to side. "It's more than that."

She glanced a Dom, who smiled encouragingly for her to continue. "I'm happier doing things on my own. I break rules. I don't conform. And I want to do those things without having to worry I'm damaging AW and the reputation you've built."

A frown creased Allegra's brow. "I still don't get it. You've had carte blanche at AW for years. We wouldn't be where we are without your research skills and innovative ideas."

"Dom has offered me a role as his sole PR consultant, and I want to take it." Zoe leaned into him, grateful for his supporting arm. "I want to fly solo. Do my own thing. I hope you understand?"

Sadness tinged with admiration clouded her friend's eyes. "'Course I do. But you invested a packet to start up AW. I won't let you leave without a generous payout."

"I don't need the money—"

"I'm not taking no for an answer," Allegra said, her firm tone brooking no argument.

"And I'm sorry to leave you in the lurch with the Kaluna campaign—"

"Don't worry about it. Molly can step into the breach."

Zoe's eyebrows rose. "Mousy Molly?"

Allegra nodded, thoughtful. "You'd be surprised. I've been hearing good things about her since she's been holding down the fort in LA. Maybe I'll even send her to scout Kaluna's Caribbean location for the next leg of the ad campaign."

"Good for her." Zoe had always liked the bookworm who preferred working on campaigns from behind the sanctity of her cubicle rather than joining the team to brainstorm. "And thanks for understanding, hon."

"What's to understand? You're a woman in love." Allegra reached for Jett's hand. "We do crazy things."

"Living with Dom isn't so crazy." Zoe snuggled into Dom. "It's fate."

"Careful, Princess." Dom tweaked her nose. "That almost sounded romantic."

She sat upright. "What did you just call me?"

"Princess," he said, with a smug grin. "Better get used to it, because sometime in the not-too-distant future, when you're not so freaked by romance and all it entails, I might just make that title official."

Zoe's heart skipped a beat at the thought of marrying Dom. "We'll see," she said, smiling that special smile she reserved solely for him, a smile that said "I'll deal with you later, and I promise you'll like it."

"I propose a toast." Dom waited until they'd picked up their champagne flutes that a waiter had deposited while they'd been chatting. "To romance."

"To romance," they echoed, clinking glasses.

Before Zoe took a sip, she leaned in close to Dom to whisper in his ear. "You only want me to be a princess so you can be my Prince Charming."

"I've got news for you, Princess," he said, kissing her earlobe. "I charmed you into the glass slipper the first moment we met."

"Smug bastard." She playfully pushed him away.

"With you by my side? You bet." Dom kissed her to whistles and catcalls from her friends.

Zoe didn't care.

Maybe romance and falling in love and having the fairy-tale ending weren't so bad after all...

If you enjoyed **WICKED HEAT** and **WANTON HEAT**, you'll love **NOT THE MARRYING KIND.**

Excerpt from Not the Marrying Kind

If you enjoyed **WICKED HEAT** and **WANTON HEAT**, you'll love **NOT THE MARRYING KIND.**

Who said marriage had to be convenient?

LA party planner Poppy Collins has kept her side business—planning divorce parties as the Divorce Diva—under wraps, but keeping her sister's company afloat is proving tougher by the day. When a new divorce party prospect gives Poppy the opportunity to save the day and boost her bottom line, she can't pass it up. But this time, she's about to get way more than she bargained for...

Vegas golden boy Beck Blackwood knows Poppy's secret, and he's not afraid to use it to get exactly what he wants—a wife. With his reputation and corporate expansion plans on the line, the only way he can repair the damage is by getting hitched, and fast. And if blackmail is the only way to get Poppy to the altar, then so be it...

But they're in the city of high stakes, and Poppy has a few aces up her sleeve. Now it's time to find out if they're playing to win...or if they're playing for keeps.

Excerpt from Not the Marrying Kind

CHAPTER ONE

Divorce Diva Daily recommends:
Playlist: "I Will Survive" by Gloria Gaynor
Movie: He's Just Not That into You
Cocktail: Slow, Comfortable Screw

Beck Blackwood could kill them.

Every one of those uptight, conservative pricks. Beck's fingers curled into fists as he paced his office, oblivious to the million-dollar view of the Strip. He liked his office perched on the highest floor of the tallest tower in Vegas. King of the world. No other feeling beat it. Apart from sex, but he'd even given up on that while finagling every detail of this deal.

This deal... He stopped in front of his desk and slammed his fist against the prospectus, the pain not registering half as much as having a boardroom of investors hedge around his win-win deal because his company wasn't respectable enough. Translation: he wasn't respectable enough. Damn it, he thought he'd left his past behind.

He'd thought wrong. Didn't matter he rivaled the richest guys in town for penthouse space, property investments, and fast cars. Because of his lifestyle choices—single, heterosexual guy who enjoyed his freedom—and the City of Sin he chose to live in, they didn't deem him worthy. Throw in the PR disaster when his site manager was found in a compromising position with an apprentice on one of his prominent constructions recently, and the fate of Blackwood Enterprises had been sealed.

Vegas loved a scandal. Sex between a married guy and a barely eighteen-year-old girl? The press attacked. Every newspaper article had shown his building site, with his company's name boldly emblazoned with its signature cactus. Damned if the thing didn't add a phallic connotation to every word printed.

Never mind he'd fired the manager and set up counseling for the teenager if she needed it.

Excerpt from Not the Marrying Kind

Never mind he'd been working his ass off trying to recoup losses the company had sustained in the crash of 2008.

Never mind he'd spent the last eighteen months living and breathing this deal to build hotels across the country that would see company profit margins soar again.

Blackwood Enterprises had been crucified. All his hard work down the toilet because they didn't deem him good enough.

Fuck them. He'd sat in the boardroom after presenting projected statistics that would've had guys with half a brain salivating, rage simmering, as each and every one of the pompous bastards scrambled for excuses.

Too big a risk. People are still talking about your company, and not in a good way.

The face of this project needs to have solid family values. What they were basically saying was that because one of his employees screwed up and he didn't have a band on his ring finger, he wasn't good enough.

Bullshit. His intercom buzzed and he glared at it, not in the mood for interruptions, not in the mood for anything unless it involved eight signatures on the construction deal of a lifetime.

"What is it, Simone?"

"Mr. Robinson wanted to remind you about the function you're planning."

He bit back his first response—*Screw Lou.* "Tell him I'm on it."

"Will do, Mr. Blackwood."

"And I'm incommunicado for the next hour." It'd take him that long to calm down.

"Okay." The intercom fell silent and he flung himself into a chair, ready to tackle a stack of quotes. However, the requisite quick glance at his inbox stalled when he glimpsed an email, every word from Stan Walkerville punctuating his disillusionment at losing out on the deal of the century.

Beck's gut twisted. Stan, the unofficial appointed leader of the investors he'd been counting on earlier today, reiterated his disap-

Excerpt from Not the Marrying Kind

pointment they wouldn't be building the biggest chain of hotels America had ever seen.

Not half as disappointed as he was. The fortune he'd amassed meant jack if they didn't consider him reliable enough. What did the old farts expect, for him to marry to become the biggest name in construction in the country?

Frigging great, he was back to this. His foolhardy plan. It had first come to him in the meeting when the investors were delivering their verdict because of the tainted Blackwood name. He'd wanted to yell, *What the fuck do you expect me to do, pull a wife out of my ass for respectability?*

While he'd wisely kept his temper in check at the time, the dumb idea had stuck in his head like a burr, no matter how many times he dismissed it. Stupid thing was, he'd analyzed it from every angle and he kept coming back to it. He needed instant propriety to clear his company's name and get the investors on his side again.

A wife would do that. *Shit.* He re-read the email. Twice. Focused on the last line. *If circumstances change, call us. We'd love to do business.* Was it as simple as that? Get hitched? Become the best in the business? Make his dream of being the biggest in America come true?

Only one problem. Where the hell was he going to find a wife? Hating what an idiot he was for even considering getting married for business, Beck scanned the rest of the emails, eventually finding the one he was searching for.

Late last night he'd agreed to another outlandish idea. Lou Robinson, his Chief Financial Officer and oldest friend, had latched onto a crazy idea to throw a party to celebrate Lou's divorce. Worse, in an effort to get Lou refocused on the job and to ensure word didn't get out his company was promoting divorce—another black mark against it for sure—Beck had said he'd organize it. Anything to snap the usually astute CFO out of his crappy mood.

Besides, organizing some senseless party had to be better than punching the wall. It'd take his mind off the deal long enough for him to come up with a viable solution for Stan and Co. to quit stalling and

Excerpt from Not the Marrying Kind

sign. One that didn't involve shackling himself to a woman. He grimaced at the thought and as the crisp website in fuchsia font came up, he wrinkled his nose.

Divorce Diva Daily. Apart from some nifty alliteration, he had a feeling this site offered nothing but a few party favors at an exorbitant price. Not that he objected to Lou spending a fortune on exorcising his demons. Hell, he'd chip in, no matter how much it took. The faster he threw this party, the faster he could have his competent CFO back.

Beck had an agenda. Schedule a meeting with the probable charlatan running this site, organize the party, make sure Lou was back on the job Monday. To come up with a feasible Plan B to wow the investors, he needed his friend alert and focused, two things he hadn't been able to attribute to Lou in a while. Lou needed to get drunk and get laid. He'd latched onto this lame-ass party idea instead. Whatever. If a divorce party would get Lou back on track, Beck was all for it. The faster he could get this organized and happening, the better.

Against his better judgment, he started reading the diva's blog entry for today.

Top Tips for moving on:

Remove all traces of the ex from your habitat— including corny first-date memorabilia, Valentine's Day cards (commercialistic crap), all engagement and marriage photos, and barf-worthy sentimental gifts.

Beck's mouth quirked at crap and barf. A woman after his own heart.

Smells are powerful reminders. If after several wash cycles his or her stink remains, burn the item involved.

Stink? Beck eased into a smile.

Music is an excellent purging tool. Download the following and crank to full volume:

"You Oughta Know" by Alanis Morrisette
"Survivor" by Destiny's Child
"Harden My Heart" by Quarterflash

Excerpt from Not the Marrying Kind

"I'm Free" by Rolling Stones
"Goodbye Earl" by Dixie Chicks
Stock up on beverages. Whether hot chocolate or appletinis or Budweisers are your poison, make sure you have plenty. You'll need it for step 5.

Throw the party of the year. Invite your closest friends and whoop it up. Thank them for supporting you. Forget the past. Move forward.

Let Divorce Diva Daily help you help yourself.

Okay, so the ending lacked the chutzpah of the earlier tips, but he kinda liked this diva. Sure, she was touting a spiel for business, but he could see the appeal in forgetting the past and moving forward.

He'd done a stand-up job of that himself. It was what drove him every day. Making sure he earned enough money and held enough power to ensure he'd never again have to tolerate the condescending, pitiful stares of people looking down on him because he had nothing.

Growing up destitute in Checkerville ensured he'd bottled those feelings of resentment and bitterness. He had used them to great effect studying endlessly to win a scholarship to college, cramming all-nighters to ace tests, and scrimping every cent he earned in part-time jobs to buy land in Vegas just before the boom hit.

Yeah, he'd shown them all. But it was days like today, when the investors stared at him with the same condescension he'd experienced in his youth that old insecurities he thought long buried flared to life. Everyone in Vegas had a past and he'd paid his dues: self-made millionaire who'd grown up tough. He hadn't hid his past from anyone. Which made their rejection now all the more infuriating.

Annoyed at the turn his thoughts were taking, he hit the "About Us" button and scanned for the price list— nada but "Price on Application." He didn't trust POA. Price on Application gave potential shysters free rein. The last thing Lou needed now was to be shafted by a shady online company.

He checked the contact details, coming up with an email address to a faceless provider. No phone number. No address. Definitely shady.

Excerpt from Not the Marrying Kind

Like that'd stop him. With a few clicks of his mouse, he'd IM'd a PI who'd done some work for him when hiring prospective employees. Beck didn't like surprises and he didn't trust an anonymous website.

In less than five minutes he had more information. Links between the quirky divorce diva and a party planning company in Provost that had candid testimonials from an extensive list of genuine clientele.

Which made him wonder. Why wouldn't the diva capitalize on the positive PR of an established company? What did she have to hide?

Instincts told him to blow off this diva and find a legit planner, but what if Lou balked and wasted more time? Beck needed a new plan to wow the investors, and that meant having Lou back on board ASAP.

The fastest option would be to follow through with Lou's choice and get this party happening. To do that, he'd have a face-to-face meeting with the diva by the end of the day.

Then he'd focus on more important matters: like finding a quickie wife.

...

"Sleazy."

"You think?" Poppy Collins stopped scrolling through her iPod for appropriate break-up songs to add to her new blog and glared at her BFF, Ashlee.

"Divorce is painful for a lot of people. And you're making fun of it." Ashlee pointed at the computer screen where Poppy had uploaded her latest post for Divorce Diva Daily, the blog that would single-handedly save Party Hard, her sister's party planning business.

"I'm intending on making a lot of money from it," Poppy muttered, tossing her iPod on the desk and swinging her chair to face Ashlee. "Money that's going to keep you employed."

Ashlee winced. "Financials that bad?"

Excerpt from Not the Marrying Kind

"You're Sara's assistant. You tell me." Poppy hated seeing her driven, career-oriented sister in a deep depression that had almost cost her the business. She hated seeing Sara's smug, WASP ex Wayne, prancing around town in a midlife-crisis-red convertible more.

Suburban Provost on the outskirts of Los Angeles wasn't big enough for both of them, which was why Poppy had insisted that Sara recuperate at a private clinic in LA while Poppy put her freelance promotion business on hold, utilized her marketing degree, and ran the business.

Problem was, Poppy knew as much about party planning as she did about relationships: absolutely zilch.

The divorce party idea was her last stand. It had to work. Sara had lost Wayne the Pain. No way would Poppy let her lose her prized business, too. It was all Sara had left.

"But celebrating divorce is tacky," Ashlee said, her gaze drawn to the PC screen again. "We'll get crucified by every do-gooder along the western seaboard."

"That's why Divorce Diva is anonymous. Plus Sara would throw a hissy fit over the D-word, so best to keep this under the radar." Poppy tapped her temple. "Up here for thinking." She pointed at her favorite crimson pumps with the three-inch stiletto heels covered in sparkles. "Down there for dancing."

"Planning parties online is one thing. What if someone wants a one-on-one consult?" Ashlee's frown deepened.

"You're not a party planner. You're a party pooper." Poppy blew out a long breath. "One step at a time, okay?"

"I've got a bad feeling about this."

"And I've got a worse one about this." Poppy stabbed at the stack of bills teetering next to her in-tray. "This idea doesn't take off? We're history."

And Sara would lose everything. No way would she let that happen. She owed her sister. Big time.

Excerpt from Not the Marrying Kind

Ashlee made disapproving clicking noises. "But divorce is so...so..."

"Inevitable? Guaranteed? Worth celebrating?"

"Private. Painful. Devastating."

"And that's exactly why I'm doing this."

Poppy had seen what impending divorce had done to Sara. Her vibrant, career-driven sis had fallen apart when Wayne walked out, and she'd been a zombie for months, popping anti-depressants until Poppy organized a prolonged stay at the clinic, complete with on-site psychologists. Sara had made progress, but to see her listless without an ounce of spark rammed home for Poppy the fact that love came with risks. Big ones.

Despite the best medical supervision, counseling, and medication, Sara languished, rehashing every reason why her marriage had failed. Poppy could've saved her a fortune in therapy bills with the truth: Wayne was an immature asshole who'd spend his life and fortune searching for the next best thing. Guys like him were never happy with what they had for long. They grew bored. They needed shiny new toys. They kept looking for something bigger and better. Splashing their cash around, seeking vicarious thrills...but they were never truly happy. Narcissistic jerks.

When Sara was ready, Poppy would help her move on with the biggest damned divorce party she could throw. Until then, it was imperative she kept Divorce Diva a secret from her stressed-out sis. With Sara's divorce imminent, no way would she approve, and Poppy didn't want her idea scuttled before it had a chance to work. Or worse, cause a relapse when Sara had finally begun to make progress.

Poppy would do whatever it took to save Sara's business. Plenty of time later to clue Sara in—after she'd succeeded.

"Divorce parties are all about marking the end of suffering and starting fresh. We have rituals for everything else—weddings, births, deaths—why not divorce?"

Ashlee said nothing, her compressed lips and dent between her brows conveying her disapproval.

Excerpt from Not the Marrying Kind

"A new phase in life is worth celebrating." Damned straight she'd help Sara celebrate The Pain's exit. But if Ashlee didn't buy the professional spiel Poppy had concocted, prospective clients wouldn't either and that would signal the end. "Plus it can be an opportunity for the newly single to thank all the people who've stood by him or her during the ordeal."

Another thing that had torn Sara apart was losing so many of her friends, those tiresome couples who were happy to hang out with other married peeps but scattered when the couple split. What was up with that? Like friendships were expendable or based on the glittery bauble on your ring finger?

"Friends can throw a party to show their divorcing pal they're supported and not alone. Or it can be a time to vent, cry, yell, laugh, whatever, in the company of people who love you." Sara had done enough crying. Poppy would ensure she whooped it up at her divorce party. "What's so bad about that?"

"I still say it's tacky." Starry-eyed, recently engaged Ashlee would think anything tarnishing the holy sanctity of marriage was tacky. Wait until dearly beloved Craig started working nights and taking longer interstate trips and deleting text messages as soon as they pinged. Then she'd get a reality check.

"We're not promoting divorce. We're giving people the option to celebrate it once it's final." Poppy pushed a stack of literature across the desk toward Ashlee. "I've researched this thoroughly. Divorce parties are the latest and greatest. Party planners are raking it in. We have to do this—it's good business."

"I guess." Ashlee gnawed her bottom lip and darted a nervous glance at the stack of bills.

"No guesswork. Divorce Diva Daily is going to rock." Feigning confidence, Poppy interlocked her hands behind her head and leaned back.

"It better. Or we'll be back serving ice creams at Iggy's." Ashlee made a mock gagging motion and Poppy wrinkled her nose at memories of their first job in high school. Iggy had a thing for cones—of

Excerpt from Not the Marrying Kind

every variety—and often rocked up to the shop stoned out of his head, sharing the love by feeling up his employees and giving away freebies. The only reason he was still in business was customer loyalty. Provost looked after its own. Poppy hoped that kind of loyalty extended to Party Hard if her Divorce Diva Daily idea went belly-up and Sara lost everything.

"It'll work, trust me."

Ashlee perched on the desk. "Like how I trusted you with my mom's bachelorette party and we almost landed in jail?" She held up her fingers and started counting off misdemeanors. "Like how I trusted you with my secret make-out place and the entire tenth grade ended up there? Like—"

"Build a bridge, hon." Poppy grinned and waved away Ashlee's concerns, thankful her best friend was along for a ride that promised to be bumpy at best.

A smile tugged at the corners of Ashlee's mouth. "I'll get over it when you prove you've matured beyond high school."

"Hey, I'm mature."

Ashlee raised an imperious eyebrow and pointed at her desk. "You're saving a printed RPatz autographed Twilight flyer, your Gryffindor Forever stick-on tattoos are plastered everywhere, and you've been clubbing three times this week."

"I like to bust a move."

"And the rest?"

"Can never have enough sparkly vamps or Harry Potter around."

"Just make this work, okay?" Ashlee's reluctant smile turned into a full-fledged grin as she tapped the stack of bills with a magenta-tipped fingernail.

"You bet." Poppy saluted. It wasn't until Ashlee bustled out of her office that Poppy slumped in her seat, glaring at the bills like they were radioactive.

No matter how many times Divorce Diva Daily recommended songs like Stevie Nicks's "Stop Dragging Your Heart Around" or ELO's "Don't Bring Me Down," they needed parties to plan.

Excerpt from Not the Marrying Kind

First request that came in? She'd bust her ass making it the best damned divorce party ever.

No problemo.

CHAPTER TWO

Divorce Diva Daily recommends:
Playlist: "Kissing a Fool" by Michael Bublé
Movie: 10 Things I Hate About You
Cocktail: Rusty Nail

"We have a major problemo." Poppy read the email for the tenth time, wondering if she needed glasses.

She could've sworn some Vegas hotshot had demanded her presence in his office at eight p.m. today. With the promise of an impressive five-figure sum if she threw the divorce party of the year.

Like hell. She'd grown up surrounded by rich pricks who expected everyone around them to dance to the "Money, Money, Money" tune. Lucky for her, she'd quit listening to Abba a long time ago.

Having über-rich parents who were plastic surgeons to the stars had been cool when she'd wanted a pony and a jumping castle, but the gloss had worn off as she grew older, surrounded by fake schmoozing, air-kisses, and selfishness. Their complete disregard for Sara's situation, with minimal financial and emotional aid? Not surprising. If it didn't benefit them, they weren't interested.

She couldn't stand the phonies who assumed money bought class. Wayne, Sara's ex, had been a classic example: flinging his cash around to impress her sister, reeling her in, then tiring of her and moving on to the next plaything.

While Poppy hated seeing Sara so devastated, a small part of her had secretly been glad when the jerk left. Sara could do so much better than The Pain.

Excerpt from Not the Marrying Kind

Thoughts of Sara brought her back to the email and Mr. Megabucks' arrogant summons.

Poppy yearned to tell him where he could stick his cash, but that kind of money would go a long way to saving Sara's ailing business. And a mega cash injection from a bigwig could launch Divorce Diva.

But was this guy for real? Eight today? On his private jet? With twenty-grand on the table?

Damn, he was seriously testing her vow to stay anonymous to protect Sara from anything remotely associated with divorce.

"What's the problem?" Ashlee squinted at the email over her shoulder. "Sounds perfectly legit to me." She rolled her eyes. "If you believe in the Tooth Fairy."

"Gave up on fairy tales a long time ago, Ash, which is why this sounds fishy. Not to mention the anonymity factor to protect Sara." She jabbed at the computer screen. "Email only? No one-on-one consultations? Any of this ringing a bell?"

"Told you this diva business would come back to bite you on the butt." Ashlee smirked.

"Yeah, that's you, a regular glass-half-full kinda gal."

Ashlee ignored her sarcasm as Poppy's gaze returned to that twenty grand. Maybe she could make an exception this one time and get Mr. Megabucks to sign a confidentiality agreement to keep her identity secret? That way she'd score the cash and protect Sara. Bonus.

"Did you look him up?"

"Just about to." Poppy typed "Beck Blackwood" into the search engine and almost flipped when an image of the guy popped up on her screen.

"Holy hotties," Ashlee muttered, shouldering her aside to take a closer look. "You're getting on that plane, right?"

"It's a jet," Poppy said, amazed she managed to string three words together without drooling all over her keyboard.

"Jet, schmet, you're going."

Excerpt from Not the Marrying Kind

The longer Poppy stared at the Gerard Butler–lookalike, the harder it was to come up with a valid reason why she shouldn't.

Unruly caramel curls. Cut-glass jaw. Intense green eyes. Rugged and raw and potent. Holy hottie, indeed.

"It's twenty big ones. You can't not go."

Good point. But the longer Poppy stared at Beck Blackwood's picture, the harder it was to ignore the squirm of butterflies unfolding their wings and getting ready to hold a rave in her belly.

"I hate when hotshots snap their fingers and expect everyone around them to jump."

Ashlee snorted. "For him, I'd jump to the moon and back if he asked."

"Shouldn't you be blinded to hot guys? Engaged bliss and all that crap?" Poppy smiled and pointed at Ashlee's glittering one-and-a-half carat pear-shaped yellow diamond.

"I'm engaged, not dead." Ashlee hid her hand behind her back and pointed at the screen with her other. "And that guy's hot enough to make any woman forget her name, let alone impending marital status."

Poppy had to agree. Didn't mean it changed a thing. She needed to maintain anonymity for Sara's sake, and despite the substantial cash temptation, she had to decline.

The phone rang and Ashlee darted off to answer it, leaving Poppy to compose a polite refusal.

Dear Mr. Blackwood, Thanks for your offer but I'm unable to accept at this time.

All the best with your party planning endeavors, The team at Divorce Diva Daily.

Poppy fired off the email, satisfied with the perfect combination of courteous and gracious. Establishing distance with the signoff had been a stroke of genius, too. How could he get uptight against an entire "team"?

About to file away his email and give in to a hankering for a

Excerpt from Not the Marrying Kind

double-shot caramel latte at the café next door, her hand hovered over the mouse to shut down her inbox when a response pinged.

Surprised—she hadn't expected to hear from him again at all, let alone so fast—she opened the email. And nearly fell off her chair.

Dear Diva, Our meeting tonight is an order, not a request.

I assume you have good reason to maintain your anonymity, so if you value your association with Party Hard I'll expect your arrival at 8 p.m. Sharp.

Beck Blackwood.

She read the email twice to make sure she wasn't hallucinating.

"Son of a bitch," she muttered, knuckling her eyes before refocusing and reading a third time. The jerk was blackmailing her. Worse, he knew about Party Hard. Freaking hell. She reined in her first urge to fire back a short, sharp retort—along the lines of "F-off"—and tried to think this through. If he hadn't pissed her off enough with his high and mighty summons before, his arrogant response to her refusal would've done it.

Who the hell did he think he was, giving her an order? Someone needed to tell him the King of Vegas had died a long time ago.

And he was a smartass, too, deliberately calling her a "diva," implying her behavior was such.

Well, she'd give him diva behavior. In person. Not because she acquiesced to blackmail, but for the simple reason she wanted to see the rich jerk's face when she told him where he could stick his offer.

Her gaze landed on the stack of unpaid bills stuffed into a fuchsia folder and her heart sank.

Who was she kidding? She couldn't afford to knock back twenty grand, not when Party Hard—and Sara—teetered on the brink. And now her number one reason for not meeting him face to face, to protect Sara's anonymity and any association with Divorce Diva Daily, had just evaporated.

Typical. When it came to money, guys like him wouldn't pay up until they knew whom they were dealing with, so it stood to reason he'd probably flung some cash around to investigate her.

Excerpt from Not the Marrying Kind

The problem was, how much did he know? And could she get him to keep his big mouth shut?

Her pride may have demanded she tell Blackwood to shove it, but her loyalty to Sara insisted she had better make this the pitch of her life.

Damn him. Once she'd sent her terse reply—*See you at eight, Poppy Collins*—she kicked the trashcan. Hard.

Ashlee stuck her head around the doorway. "Everything okay?"

"Fine," Poppy said, glaring at Blackwood's pic that popped up on her screen when she closed her inbox. Bad move. She should've shut down the search engine first, as Ashlee wolf-whistled when she sauntered over to the desk.

"Better than fine, getting up close and personal with 'The Hottie.' " Ashlee made puckering noises and Poppy swatted her away.

She didn't want to explain the online altercation with Blackwood or his attempt at blackmail. Ash would worry, so Poppy decided to play the casual game. She'd handle Beck Blackwood herself.

"I'm pretty sure I won't be getting that close to potentially our biggest—and only—client at this stage, but in case I do, I'll let you know how his technique rates."

"That's my girl." Ashlee slugged her on the arm. "You know you'll be staying overnight in Vegas, right?"

"Hadn't planned to."

"Guys like that will have a hotel room ready and waiting for you." Ashlee spoke slowly, as if Poppy had suddenly developed obtuseness. "He's sending a private jet. What's one little hotel room for the night?"

Now that she'd decided to go, Poppy hadn't counted on a layover, but considering it'd be late when she finished her pitch, maybe she should pack for an overnighter just in case.

"Silk."

"What?"

"Bet The Hottie favors silk lingerie." Ashlee tapped her bottom lip, pondering. "Maybe lace?"

Excerpt from Not the Marrying Kind

Annoyed by the thought of wearing anything remotely sexy near Beck Blackwood, Poppy waved Ashlee away. "Haven't you got work to do?"

"Yeah, but bet it's not half as fun as your work tonight." Ashlee blew her a kiss as she headed for the door. "And here's another tip. When in Vegas, always bet on black."

"I'm not gambling—"

"Black silk, satin, lace, whatever. LBD, push-up bra, stockings, you'll have him throwing the big bucks at you."

"Dressed like that, it won't be for my party planning skills," Poppy muttered, earning a grin from Ashlee.

"Good luck, hon." Ashlee gave her a thumbs-up sign before heading back to her desk in the outer office.

Poppy didn't need luck. She'd prove to moneybags Blackwood she could match it with the big boys in Vegas and throw a party the city would never forget. Failure wasn't an option.

As for the laid-back, rugged, gorgeous thing he had going on? She'd wear her white cotton, purple polka-dot granny panties to the meeting. It paid to not tempt fate, and considering the dry spell she'd had for the last eight months while juggling Sara's depression and business, she wouldn't want her panties getting any ideas and sliding off at the first sight of those penetrating green eyes.

Yeah, she'd head to this meeting in Vegas well prepared. Beck Blackwood wouldn't know what hit him.

...

"Make mine a double."

"You've had enough." Beck shook his head and slid the aged whiskey out of Lou's reach. "Time to call it a night."

"You're no fun." Lou glared at him through slightly glazed eyes, spoiling his mean look by semi-sliding off the stool. "I know why, too. It's because those investors screwed us this morning."

Beck reassessed. Lou couldn't be completely hammered if he was astute enough to home in on the one reason behind Beck's foul mood. But the last thing Beck felt like doing was rehashing this morning. Not while bitterness still burned his gut.

"Wanna know what I think?" Lou slammed a hand on the table, making the whiskey glasses clink. "Screw the investors. And screw Julie, the money-hungry, soul-sucking, bee-yatch—"

"Come on, big boy, time for bed." Beck had to interject before Lou launched on another abusive tirade. He'd never liked Lou's ex, but Julie didn't deserve the crap Lou was heaping on her. They'd both screwed up and divorce had been inevitable. Beck could've told him so at the start and saved them both the angst and a small fortune slugging it out via lawyers.

Marriage was the pits. And then you divorced. Simple equation. Which was why he avoided doing the math.

Beck slid a hand under Lou's elbow to help him up, but his friend shrugged him off with surprising force.

"Screw you. I wanna party."

Dragging in a deep breath, Beck mentally counted to ten. He didn't have time for this. He had to meet with the party planner at eight, and considering it was now seven, he was done babysitting. "I'm meeting with your planner soon, so save your partying for next weekend."

"Been a long time since I partied hard." Lou slumped lower in his chair. "A ball and chain does that to a guy. Next weekend...yeah, sounds good..." Lou's gaze focused on the muted TV over Beck's shoulder, eyes narrowed as he leaned forward. "Turn that up."

Beck glanced at his watch, groaned, and stabbed at the volume button on the remote in time to catch the end of a segment on divorce parties from a well-respected current-affairs show.

"See? Told you throwing a party to celebrate my freedom is cool." Lou leaped from his chair, staggered a little, before gaining his balance. "I'm a friggin' genius."

Debatable, as Beck took in Lou's crumpled shirt, unkempt trousers, and rumpled jacket.

Excerpt from Not the Marrying Kind

But the faster he appeased his friend, the faster he'd get him off to bed so he could meet the planner and tick one more thing off his extensive to-do list.

"I'll hash out the details tonight and fill you in tomorrow."

"Maybe I should come with you? Help plan?" Lou peered at him through bleary eyes and Beck knew if the party planner took one look at him she'd re-board the jet for LA. "I can help. Divorce parties are hip, all the celebs are doing it. Even the local business journal and CNN said so."

Beck couldn't give a shit whether the President himself approved of divorce parties. He needed to appease Lou so he could get this thing done and move onto more important matters, like planning his next line of attack with the investors. And finding himself a wife.

"So you checked out that website link I gave you?" Before Beck could bundle him toward the nearest elevator, Lou had whipped out his smartphone and brought up Divorce Diva Daily, grinning inanely as he peered at the website. "Yep, I'm going to get me a little divorce diva to throw the biggest damned party Vegas has ever seen."

"Got it. Big party. I'll tell her."

"I'll come meet her—"

"No."

Lou finally picked up on the *Don't jerk me around* intonation, and nodded. "Okay. But this party has to be mega." He threw his arms wide. "I want the whole goddamn town to know nobody gets to stick it to Lou Robinson."

"Leave it to me—"

"I need closure." Lou gripped Beck's arm in a surprisingly strong grasp for a near-teetotaler who'd downed three quarters of a bottle of whiskey. "You'll take care of this, right?"

Casting a dubious glance at the website, Beck nodded.

"You know what you need?" Lou jabbed a finger at the website. "The opposite of this."

Beck had to drag Lou to the elevator. Fast.

"You need a wife." Lou grinned like he'd single-handedly solved

Excerpt from Not the Marrying Kind

the world's El Niño crisis. "Those investors think Blackwood Enterprises is trash? Show them you're not."

The fact his inebriated friend had inadvertently echoed his irrational thoughts from earlier didn't help Beck's mood. "Yeah, maybe I should ask this divorce party chick for marital advice or a fix-up."

"Can't be any worse than this morning." Lou winced. "Smug bastards. Hate uptight pricks like that."

Beck couldn't agree more.

"Maybe the divorce diva runs a dating site, too?" Lou snapped his fingers. "Instant wifey."

"You're insane." Besides, Beck had already thoroughly researched the diva and she didn't moonlight as a matchmaker. Her terse reply to his email summons had made him laugh. What did she think, that he'd go into a face-to-face consult unprepared? Would be interesting what she came up with when he confronted her. Would she scuttle him with BS or tell the truth?

"Drunk and insane," Beck amended.

"You have to admit, the chick has style." Lou chuckled as he scanned the diva's website and Beck couldn't help but take a look. The fact that she'd made him laugh with her first blog entry? A one-off.

BURN BABY BURN The physical fallout from a marriage break-up can be the pits. Reminders of your ex everywhere you turn, from old razors lurking in bathroom cabinets to slash unsuspecting fingers, to ratty T-shirts with obnoxious slogans you once tolerated all in the name of love (barf!).

He snickered.

Divorce Diva Daily's advice today is "Burn, baby, burn." A burning ceremony can be cathartic. You may like to burn:

Your marriage certificate

A list of things you won't miss (e.g., remote control hogging, snoring, neuroses á la "Do I look fat in this?", make-up remnants from the sixties, etc.)

Photos

Excerpt from Not the Marrying Kind

A replica of the ex's privates
All of the above
A burning ritual signifies letting go, a proactive way to move on. And if you can't burn, flushing or shredding works just as effectively.

Beck found himself grinning inanely and Lou sniggered. She'd done it again. Made him laugh. Something he didn't do much of these days.

It made him all the more curious about the woman who'd answered his email. He had no idea if Poppy Collins was the divorce diva or an underling, but considering she'd be in his office in an hour, he'd soon find out. Everyone had a weak spot.

He'd learned that the hard way. It was why he abhorred weakness of any kind, why he'd developed a hard outer shell by the time he hit preschool. Being raised by Pa had toughened him, but he had his absentee parents to thank for teaching him the art of indifference from an early age.

Before they shot up and killed themselves, that is.

"If she's this cool in real life, my party's going to rock." Lou swiped his finger across the smartphone, squinting his eyes to read the fine print. "Did you see the links to high-profile business mags and journals? Even CBS Los Angeles reported divorce parties are the latest, greatest thing."

"Saw that. Also saw the part where it said divorce party planners are doing brisk business and raking in healthy profits."

"You're a cynic." Lou glanced up, the hint of vulnerability in his blurry eyes making Beck feel like a bastard.

Lou was going through a rough time. The least he could do was be supportive.

Who knew misery paid? These parties may be about consoling and support and celebrating a new life phase, but to Beck, they reeked of sadness and bitterness and anger. Then again, Lou had been moping around, his mind not one hundred percent focused on work, so if this dumb divorce party purged his blues, Beck was all for it.

Excerpt from Not the Marrying Kind

"Pays to be cautious, my friend."

"Bet you researched this diva." Lou snorted. "You vet everybody."

"I checked into her." And found nothing telling. A private Facebook page Beck couldn't access, a few articles she'd written for a high school newspaper in suburban Provost, no pictures. Damn.

After the PI had given him the link between Divorce Diva Daily and a respectable party planning company in Provost, he'd wanted more on the would-be charlatan. He'd come up with nothing. Her initial refusal to meet surprised him. Money talked, and he'd expected the twenty grand he'd dangled as incentive to meet him would serve its purpose.

Interesting. For someone hiding behind a computer screen, his jab at revealing her links to Party Hard had been more of an enticement to meet than the money.

Why? What did the divorce diva have to hide? And did it involve screwing over her customers? Too bad for her the one thing he enjoyed as much as accumulating a fortune was solving mysteries.

And she'd just moved to the top of his to-do list. "Come on, big fella, time to get you to bed so I can go organize this rockin' party."

"You're the best," Lou mumbled, shrugging off Beck's attempt at help and staggering toward the elevator.

Not yet, he wasn't, but Beck intended on being the best. When he secured the nationwide deal, he'd prove it.

CHAPTER THREE

Divorce Diva Daily recommends:
Playlist: "You Give Love a Bad Name" by Bon Jovi
Movie: Something's Gotta Give
Cocktail: Fallen Angel

As the jet touched down in Vegas, Poppy wriggled in her seat, craning for a better view.

She loved this town. Loved the glitz and glamor, the razzle-

Excerpt from Not the Marrying Kind

dazzle, the surrealism of not sleeping if you didn't want to. She'd visited twice, once with Ashlee after they'd graduated high school and another time with a guy she'd been seeing for a month.

The first time she'd shopped and done the shows circuit and partied her way through the three days with Ashlee. The second time, she drank her way through the weekend when the guy turned out to be a gambling fiend who had ditched her to play blackjack.

This visit promised to be very different. As the jet taxied along the runway, she glanced at her surroundings, impressed despite her snit with its owner.

Butter-soft leather recliners the color of ripe wheat lined one side of the jet, directly opposite a mahogany bar with forest green leather bar stools edging it. The flat-screen TV above the bar was larger than her bedroom back home. Squishy ochre cushions placed strategically on the chairs highlighted their pristine lushness, while the mahogany coffee tables were so highly polished she could have used them as mirrors.

The opulent luxury made her feel like she'd stumbled into a princess' dream. And that was before she'd been personally served a late lunch of sesame-crusted tempura shrimp served with a watercress and pear salad, rose-stewed figs and baklava, and hand-squeezed lemonade by a steward. She would've preferred to take him up on his offer of Moët, but she needed her faculties clear and functioning for her meeting with Beck Blackwood. For all she knew, it might be a ploy to get her tipsy so he could take advantage of her. A girl could dream, right?

As the jet's only other occupant, the steward had been attentive yet deferent, and Poppy had almost wished Beck Blackwood had summoned her to Miami.

She could get used to this. Her parents were loaded, but they weren't rich enough for private jets. First class had been a bonus. She despised the fakeness of the moneyed social circles she'd been raised in, but when it came to flying? Tattoo a giant "H" on her forehead for "hypocrite."

Excerpt from Not the Marrying Kind

"Traffic is backed up on the ground, Miss Collins, so you'll be disembarking in ten minutes."

"Thanks." She smiled at the steward, who tipped his cap before easing behind the door at the rear of the plane. Ten minutes gave her time to do a quick blog update before prepping the pitch of her life.

She'd just fired up her tablet when the phone on the bar rang.

She ignored it, until the steward stuck his head around the back partition. "That'll be for you, Miss Collins."

"Who—" But he'd already vanished and with a sinking feeling, she headed for the phone. Only one person would be calling her on a private jet. *His* private jet.

Great. The plane had barely touched down and Mr. Megabucks was already expecting her to jump to his tune. Billionaires and their blasted foibles.

She hit Answer on the phone. "Poppy Collins speaking."

A long pause made the hairs on the nape of her neck snap to attention.

"Hope you're quicker off the mark with your pitch than you are answering phones."

Hot damn. She knew he had the look, and now she knew he had the voice to go with it. Deep. Resonant. Commanding. With an edge of huskiness that suggested all-night sex with no regrets.

A host of smartass retorts sprung to Poppy's lips, but she clamped the urge to use them. If Beck Blackwood was serious about the offer of twenty big ones, she couldn't afford to piss him off. Time enough for that later, after he'd signed on the dotted line.

"I was busy going over my presentation." She injected the right amount of subservience to appease the arrogant puppet-master. "What can I do for you?"

"Sure you want me to answer that?"

Was he flirting with her? Maybe she should've fortified those granny panties. With steel.

"We're meeting shortly, Mr. Blackwood. Unless there's a point to this phone call, I'd like to get back to my presentation."

Excerpt from Not the Marrying Kind

He snickered. "Snark. Like your blog."

"You read it?"

She mentally slapped herself upside the head. Of course he would've read it. If his investigators had discovered her link to Party Hard, they probably knew everything from her preferred cereal to her cup size.

"It's entertaining in its own way." Way to go with the backhanded compliment. She should let it go. But she'd had enough of his condescension, mega payoff or not.

"In its own way?"

"For a fluff piece."

She heard the hint of amusement and it was the only thing that prevented her from telling him where he could stick his divorce party. That and the memory of the last time she'd seen Sara: pale, listless, morose, and overmedicated.

"Did my reference to your fluff piece offend you?"

He was baiting her. He wanted her to bite back. Let him wait.

"Lucky for me that fluff grabbed your attention long enough for you to fly me out here to organize a party you'll never forget."

This time he laughed out loud. "I like confidence in a woman."

"Then you'll love me." She winced, instantly regretting her sassy comeback. She didn't want any guy to love her, not in any sense. Love was for losers. Masochistic losers.

Though she shouldn't knock it, considering those losers would keep Party Hard afloat, courtesy of her Divorce Diva Daily ingenuity.

"We'll see," he said, the uncomfortable edge underlying his tone matching her squirm-factor at the remotest mention of the L-word. "See you soon."

Before she could respond, he'd hung up, leaving her perplexed as she stared at the phone. What the hell was that all about? She had no idea why he'd called, and second-guessing his motivation didn't help her burgeoning nerves.

Excerpt from Not the Marrying Kind

For despite a foolproof presentation designed to wow, she was nervous.

This had to work. For all their sakes.

Poppy smoothed her skirt and tugged at the hem of her jacket as she stepped onto the tarmac. She'd gone for understated elegance: pinstriped ebony suit with a below-knee pencil skirt, three-inch patent heels, and stockings. Her only concession to her usual flair was a crimson silk shirt that elevated the suit from prim to possibilities.

She wanted to wow Beck Blackwood. To show him she wasn't some underling who jumped when he snapped his fingers and flung his cash around, even though that was exactly what she'd done.

She squared her shoulders, tucked her satchel under her arm, and marched toward the limousine waiting nearby. In a town where limos were the norm rather than the exception, this one stood out: long, silver, shapely.

After the jet, it figured. Beck Blackwood had the best of everything and wouldn't settle for anything less. Lucky for him, she intended on being the best in the party planning business.

As she neared the limo, the back passenger door opened and a hint of premonition strummed her spine. The limo had a passenger, and with the chauffeur waiting a few discreet feet away, that passenger had to be important enough to command privacy.

Her step faltered as Beck Blackwood stepped from the limo, imposing and arresting and way too gorgeous to be legal.

Hell. When he said *See you soon* she'd assumed he'd meant his office. She hadn't expected a welcoming committee, though by his shuttered expression he was none too welcoming.

He watched her approach and her skin prickled with every step. There was nothing overtly sexual in his steady stare, but every nerve ending in her body went on high alert the closer she got.

Ashlee had labeled him a hottie. He was so far beyond hottie in the flesh it wasn't funny.

When she'd envisioned their first meeting, it had been in an office with neutral furniture and high-tech gadgets. She'd mentally

Excerpt from Not the Marrying Kind

rehearsed a hundred professional greetings for when an über secretary ushered her into that office.

Sadly, her carefully constructed vocab designed to impress deserted her the moment she got within three feet of the guy.

That pic online, the one bearing a strong resemblance to Gerard Butler? Did. Not. Do. Him. Justice.

Embarrassingly speechless, she did the only thing she could: when in doubt, smile. It must've lost something in the translation and come out an inane grin, because his eyebrow inverted in a comical WTF.

"Nice blouse."

She raised him a WTF eyebrow in return. Of all the introductions she'd imagined, that hadn't been one of them, a strangely intimate comment on her attire.

He was trying to disarm her. It was working. Not that she'd let him know. "Nice tie."

To her surprise he laughed. "Touché."

"Was the color a deliberate choice?" She often wore a touch of deep crimson—poppy—as a good-luck token, hence her shirt.

He slid a finger beneath the tie's knot, loosening it a tad. It didn't detract from his smooth shark aura. He'd probably gone for a shot-silk poppy tie to goad her. "Poppy seems to be a popular color these days."

She didn't want to ask how he knew that. He probably had a slew of glam girlfriends in slinky, revealing, poppy dresses for every day of the week. The good thing about their absurd color conversation: it gave her time to gather her wits. Time to get this meeting off to a better start.

"Now that we've analyzed this year's most sought-after color for Fashion Week, should we get down to business?" She held out her hand. "Poppy Collins. Pleased to meet you."

"Beck Blackwood. Likewise." The moment his large hand enveloped hers, she stiffened against the unexpected zap that sizzled up her arm and centered on places it had no right centering.

Excerpt from Not the Marrying Kind

If she didn't know better, she could've sworn the zap worked both ways, as his pupils widened perceptibly and he quickly released her.

"Call me Beck."

She inclined her head. "Call me stupid."

His eyes widened in surprise and she mentally clapped a hand over her mouth. Too late.

"For agreeing to meet you despite your less than subtle attempt at blackmail?"

His sinful mouth eased into a smirk. One she'd like to wipe off. "Don't take it personally. I vet all the people I hire." The smirk gave way to a practiced smile. "Pays to be alert in any business, as I'm sure you'd appreciate."

Great. Was he saying she was an astute businesswoman, or warning her to be on her guard? Whatever. She'd come this far, no point alienating him. This party would launch Divorce Diva Daily, and if Hotshot could keep his mouth shut about her identity, this could prove a win-win all around.

"Just so you know, I'm flexible professionally but I don't take orders kindly."

"Noted." That damned smile widened. "Have to say, you're not what I expected." His all-encompassing stare started at her patent pumps and swept upward, coolly assessing, as she crazily wished it'd linger in those places his handshake had zapped a second ago.

"Let me guess. You were expecting bitter and twisted?"

"Would you settle for wary and cynical?"

Not fair. Not only was the guy gorgeous, he had the intelligence and quick wit to match.

"Not married?" His gaze dipped to her ring finger.

"No way," she said, immediately regretting her instinctive outburst under his intense scrutiny.

He had the penetrating stare down pat and she could easily imagine him facing off a boardroom full of adversaries.

She wasn't so easily intimidated. "No engagements, no significant

Excerpt from Not the Marrying Kind

others, no cramping of style." She waved her left hand in his face to prove it.

"And you've got plenty of that." His stare softened into something she didn't dare label.

She preferred the intimidating stare to the admiration tinged with a hint of heat.

"Let's go. We've got a lot of work to do." He reverted to brusque and abrupt, and she preferred it. The less zapping that occurred around Beck, the better. Even thinking of him on a first-name basis implied an intimacy she didn't like.

"After you." He gestured toward the open limo door, his hand brushing the small of her back in gentle guidance.

Yep, the zap was still there. Disconcerting and disarming. She slid into the limo. The sooner she nailed this pitch, the sooner she could head back to the safety of Provost and the anonymity of Divorce Diva Daily.

This was one diva that had no intention of flaunting anything.

...

Beck sprawled across the seat opposite Poppy, watching her type furiously on her tablet. No hardship, watching her.

He liked the fact she was ignoring him. It meant he had her rattled.

Join the club. She'd shot down his expectations of a dour, bitter, forty- something, middle-aged divorcée the moment she stepped onto the tarmac and he got his first look at the pocket dynamo.

Because that's what she was, fire and ice wrapped in a delicious, petite package. He hadn't banked on the uncharacteristic, almost visceral reaction and it unnerved him.

He'd expected sour and acrimonious, not sizzling and defiant. And her damned voice: rich, teasing, tempting. Brought to mind visions of smoky nightclubs, smooth bourbon, and sultry nights made for sex.

Excerpt from Not the Marrying Kind

That's what annoyed him the most. He never mixed business with pleasure, and the fact she made him think of sex had him re-evaluating the wisdom of meeting with her. He should've thrown cash at her online and let her do her worst.

The snark didn't help, either. He liked feisty, a woman to challenge him. He'd never found one yet. Once they discovered who he was, women tended to accede to his judgment or attempt to sway him with vamp factor. Both plays grew tiresome after a while.

Poppy was neither. She'd confronted him about his email demand and issued a subtle warning she wouldn't put up with it again. He admired her bluntness. It bode well for getting this party happening ASAP.

She was definitely the diva behind the website—it didn't take long for her natural impudence to surface in person. And it was a better aphrodisiac than any near-naked showgirl. Or naked one, for that matter.

The instant she'd started matching wits with him, he'd been turned on. Go figure.

He preferred his business dealings to be hard-on free and the fact she'd crept under his guard rankled. He didn't have time for distractions.

"Problem?" She pinned him with a narrow-eyed glare.

"No."

Discounting the one where he couldn't take his eyes off her. He'd bet his last dollar that crimson silk shirt with a hint of cleavage was the real her, bold and flamboyant, and she'd been unable to resist hiding her true self behind a business suit designed to impress.

He was impressed, all right, but it had more to do with the whole package than her suit. Not strictly beautiful, but she had an inherent fire that made her caramel eyes glow with that indefinable something that turned guys' heads.

Heart-shaped face, pert nose, slightly wider than average mouth—he wouldn't go there—shoulder-length layered just-out-of-bed

Excerpt from Not the Marrying Kind

brown hair equaled a striking combination, and that was on top of her enticing curves.

So he was attracted to her. Big deal. Didn't mean he'd act on it.

"Didn't your mother ever tell you it's rude to stare?"

And just like that, his hard-on deflated. "Before or after she overdosed on coke?"

Stricken, she paled and he silently cursed. "Sorry."

"Don't be, I'm not."

He'd given up mourning his parents—or lack of—a long time ago. Wasted energy. His folks had never given a damn about him, had indulged in the selfish lifestyle of druggies who didn't care about anything except their next hit, neglecting their kid in the process.

He'd attended their funerals out of obligation and respect for Pa, who'd been as stoic as him. The Blackwoods were confirmed realists, what was left of the family. Beck respected straight shooting, and Pa was one of the best at it. To this day, Beck believed he'd got into so many fistfights as a kid just so he could listen to Pa dole out his dry commentary on life as he patched him up.

It'd been too long since he'd visited Pa. He'd rectify that once this deal went through.

He glanced out the window as the limo eased along the Strip, the twinkling lights and streaming crowds a comfort. He preferred desert silence over big-city bedlam, but every time he cruised through this town, he knew he'd made it.

Size mattered in Vegas, and he'd gone all out when he'd made his first millions, gambling on property investments rather than slots, ensuring every single person who'd ever doubted him sat up and took notice. Blackwood Enterprises was renowned for its luxury constructions, and he intended for everyone in America to know it.

He gestured out the window. "Been to Vegas before?"

"Twice." She wrinkled her nose.

"You don't like it?"

"It's okay if you like flashy."

Excerpt from Not the Marrying Kind

"Don't be fooled by the glitz. If you look beneath the surface, there's more on offer."

She eyeballed him and he didn't know what made him more edgy—her ability to undermine him with a glance or the strange feeling she could see down to his soul. "We're talking about the city, right?" Damn, she was good.

"Of course. Making idle chitchat."

"I have a feeling you never say anything without an end game in sight."

There she went again, pinning him down with an intuition that left him squirming.

He'd aimed to make her uncomfortable by picking her up from the airport. He didn't appreciate having the tables turned.

Time to have a little fun. "We're almost there." He half expected her to call him on his abrupt change of topic and his gruffness. Instead, she sat there, staring at him, silently appraising.

Yeah, definitely time to regain control. "I hope you packed a change of clothes along with your presentation?" He pointed to her giant satchel.

"Why?" The first flicker of uncertainty had her glancing at the bag with the barest of frowns.

"Because you're staying the night. With me."

To read on, **NOT THE MARRYING KIND** is available online, along with all of Nicola's fun, flirty books.

FREE book and more

SIGN UP TO NICOLA'S NEWSLETTER for a free book!

Read Nicola's newest feel-good romance **DID NOT FINISH**

Or her new gothic **THE RETREAT**

Try the **CARTWRIGHT BROTHERS** duo

FASCINATION

PERFECTION

The **WORKPLACE LIAISONS** duo

THE BOSS

THE CEO

Try the **BASHFUL BRIDES** series

NOT THE MARRYING KIND

NOT THE ROMANTIC KIND

NOT THE DARING KIND

NOT THE DATING KIND

The **CREATIVE IN LOVE** series

THE GRUMPY GUY

THE SHY GUY

THE GOOD GUY

Try the **BOMBSHELLS** series

BEFORE (FREE!)

BRASH

BLUSH

BOLD

BAD

BOMBSHELLS BOXED SET

The **WORLD APART** series

WALKING THE LINE (FREE!)

CROSSING THE LINE

TOWING THE LINE

BLURRING THE LINE

WORLD APART BOXED SET

The **HOT ISLAND NIGHTS** duo

WICKED NIGHTS

WANTON NIGHTS

The **BOLLYWOOD BILLIONAIRES** series

FAKING IT

MAKING IT

The **LOOKING FOR LOVE** series

LUCKY LOVE

CRAZY LOVE

SAPPHIRES ARE A GUY'S BEST FRIEND

THE SECOND CHANCE GUY

Check out Nicola's website for a full list of her books.

And read her other romances as Nikki North.

'MILLIONAIRE IN THE CITY' series.

LUCKY

COCKY

CRAZY

FANCY

FLIRTY

FOLLY

MADLY

Check out the **ESCAPE WITH ME** series.

DATE ME

LOVE ME

DARE ME

TRUST ME

FORGIVE ME

Try the **LAW BREAKER** series

THE DEAL MAKER
THE CONTRACT BREAKER

About the Author

USA TODAY bestselling and multi-award winning author Nicola Marsh writes page-turning fiction to keep you up all night.
She's published 80 books and sold 8 million copies worldwide.
She currently writes contemporary romance and domestic suspense.
She's also a Waldenbooks, Bookscan, Amazon, iBooks and Barnes & Noble bestseller, a RBY (Romantic Book of the Year) and National Readers' Choice Award winner, and a multi-finalist for a number of awards including the Romantic Times Reviewers' Choice Award, HOLT Medallion, Booksellers' Best, Golden Quill, Laurel Wreath, and More than Magic.
A physiotherapist for thirteen years, she now adores writing full time, raising her two dashing young heroes, sharing fine food with family and friends, and her favorite, curling up with a good book!